Tom Taylor, A. Dubourg

New Men and Old Acres

A Comedy, in Three Acts

Tom Taylor, A. Dubourg

New Men and Old Acres
A Comedy, in Three Acts

ISBN/EAN: 9783337054649

Printed in Europe, USA, Canada, Australia, Japan

Cover: Foto ©Andreas Hilbeck / pixelio.de

More available books at **www.hansebooks.com**

NEW MEN AND OLD ACRES.

A Comedy.

IN THREE ACTS.

By TOM TAYLOR AND A. DUBOURG,

Author of "A Sister's Penance," "Henry Dunbar," "Mary Warner," "Plot and Passion," "The Hidden Hand," etc., etc.

AS FIRST PERFORMED AT THE THEATRE ROYAL, MANCHESTER FRIDAY, AUG. 20, 1869, AND AT THE HAYMARKET THEATRE, LONDON, UNDER THE MANAGEMENT OF J. B. BUCK-STONE, ESQ., ON MONDAY, OCTOBER 25, 1869.

TO WHICH IS ADDED

A DESCRIPTION OF THE COSTUMES—CAST OF THE CHARACTERS—EN-
TRANCES AND EXITS—RELATIVE POSITIONS OF THE PER-
FORMERS ON THE STAGE, AND THE WHOLE
OF THE STAGE BUSINESS

———

NEW YORK:
ROBERT M. DE WITT, PUBLISHER,
No. 13 FRANKFORT STREET.

CAST OF CHARACTERS.

Haymarket Theatre,
London, Oct. 25, 1869.

Marmaduke Vavasour, Esq. (of Cleve Abbey)...........Mr. CHIPPENDALE.
Samuel brown (a Liverpool Merchant)..................Mr. HOWE.
Mr. Bunter (a Self-made Man).........................Mr. BUCKSTONE.
Blazenbarg (a Mining Agent and Financier)............Mr. ROGERS.
Bertie Fitzurse......................................Mr. BUCKSTONE, Jr.
Seeker (an Attorney).... ....Mr. BRAID.
Gantry (Butler at Cleve Abbey).......................Mr. WEATHERSBY.
Tollit (Clerk of the Works)..........................Mr. JAMES.
Lady Mildred Vavasour................................Mrs. CHIPPENDALE.
Lilian Vavasour......................................Miss MADGE ROBERTSON.
Mrs. Bunter......... ....Mrs. E. FITZWILLIAM.
Fanny Bunter...Miss CAROLINE HILL.
Mrs. Brill (Housekeeper at Cleve Abbey)..............Miss HARRISON.

SCENERY—(*English, modern*).

ACT I.—(No change). Library in an old castle, modernized. Wainscotting, and painted ceiling in 5th grooves.

..........Backing.

Closed in.

Antique furniture. Carpet down, representing marquetry flooring. Silver plate on sideboard, L. 2 E. French bow-window R. C. in flat. View of ruined Abbey on 4th groove flat. Alcove L. U. corner has the library book-shelves. A window in L. 3 E. set, with stained glass, armorial bearings. Stained glass shields on the upper part of window in F. Gilt and white knobs to each centre of the octagons in ceiling pattern, the ceiling covering the stage. Sunlight effect R. U. F. Books and photographic album on table.

ACT II.—(No change) Ruins of Abbey in 4th or 5th groove. Archway C, in 3d or 4th groove; set walls. Archways L. and R.; ruined windows. Tree wings and sinks. Ivy trailings. Flowers, some to pick, R. 1 E. Rustic table L., with chairs, chair and rustic settee R. Afternoon sun. View of castellated mansion, R. C., on flat, among trees.

ACT III.—(No change). Drawing-room in 4th groove. All very showy and bright. Gilt furniture. Many pictures in large frames. Parian statuettes under glass about stage, and on gilt round tables R. and L. front. Gilt and ebony etageres at corners up R. and L. R. 1 and 2 E. open for a French window, opening into conservatory, some of the flowers and plants of which are shown. Doors L. 1 and 2 E. Lace and other curtains to windows. Ceiling closed in, with stained glass skylight at C., 2d entrance line. Table L. C. front, with chairs. Sofa R. C. front, with small table. Flower baskets on stands each side of window, R. Life-size statues, nymphs, each side of D. in F., in upper entrance, with smaller statues behind them, to give the illusion of diminishing by perspective, instead of showing that they are *really* smaller. Writing materials on L. table.

COSTUMES.—(English, present day.)

SAMUEL BROWN.—Aged about thirty-five. Close shaven, but small side-whiskers. *Act I.:* Black hat and coat, gray pants. *Act II.:* Walking-dress, black coat, light pants, white vest, black high-crown felt hat. *Act III.:* Black coat and vest, dark gray pants. Enters with black valise, papers in his pocket.

BUNTER.—Affects a semi-clerical air; sanctimonious in voice and manner. Black coat, white cravat, black vest, gray pants.

VAVASOUR.—Old Man. Gray Whiskers, white hair. *Act I.:* White vest, black coat, light gray pants, eye-glass on black ribbon, watch chain, cravat of dark blue silk with white spots. *Act II.:* Black suit, drab hat with broad black band, cane, gloves on. *Act III.:* Walking-dress, all black, hat as before.

BLAZENBAIG.—A German, speaking broken English. Heavy beard and moustache. High black, soft felt hat, cutaway coat, vest and pants of russet velveteen, watch-chain. *Act II.:* Enters with fisherman's basket hung over his shoulder by its strap.

BERTIE FITZURSE.—A young "Swell." *Act I.:* Tweed suit. *Act II.:* Gray tweed suit, short coat, black Tyrolese hat with cock's feathers. *Act III.:* Same as last; flower in coat buttonhole.

SECKER.—Black, black gloves, neck-cloth, side-whiskers.

GANTRY.—A Butler, black suit, white tie.

TOLLIT.—Walking-dress, hat.

VALET.—To the Bunters.—Black suit.

TELEGRAPH MESSENGER.—Blue, edged with red, cap.

LILIAN VAVASOUR.—*Act I.:* Short fashionable dress; the sash to match being up C. on table, ready to be fastened on; hair loosely flowing, like a young girl's. *Act II.:* White muslin dress, with a *very* short black silk upperskirt over it, jet ornaments. *Act III.:* Elegant walking-dress, gray hat, Elizabethan ruff.

LADY MILDRED.—(This is not an Old Woman's part but a Comedienne's, requiring an imposing appearance, if possible). *Act I.:* Rich house-dress; rich cashmere shawl, head-dress ornaments, black lace trimmings, gilt smelling-bottle. *Act II.:* Handsome walking-dress, fan, shawl wound around her like a plaid is worn, smelling-bottle, gold-mounted eye-glass. *Act III.:* Walking-dress, smelling-bottle.

MRS. BUNTER.—(Not an Old Woman's part, but a Comedienne's). Very vulgar in speech, dress and manner. *Act I.:* Showy walking-dress, of some novel color. *Act II.:* Change, walking-dress, parasol. *Act III.:* House-dress, jewelry.

FANNY BUNTER.—*Act I.:* Walking dress, showy. *Act II.:* White muslin dress. *Act III.:* Silk house-dress.

MRS. BRILL.—Plain dress, white cap, black silk apron.

PROPERTIES (See Scenery)

ACT I.—Papers on table L. front; telegraphic message; tatting for LILIAN, partly worked; reticule for MRS. BUNTER; small bouquet for FANNY BUNTER; *Act II.*: Set of instruments for croquet, the hoops being set up on stage at rise of curtain; for BLAZENBAIG, fishing basket containing pieces of stone and ore; fishing-pole, with a spear-head in the butt; a letter in an official blue envelope stamped in red with the British royal coat of arms; a dandelion flower to be plucked among other flowers R. 1 E.; letter for SECKER; telegraph message for TELEGRAPH MESSENGER; several sheets of paper, folded up, in BLAZENBAIG'S pocket. *Act III.* (*See Scenery*): writing materials on table L. front; check-book for BUNTER; lunch for one to be brought in on tray; a large sheet of parchment, the upper part containing a genealogical tree with shields on the branches, three rows of four shields in all, colored, with some fifteen lines of reading at the foot of the page; it rolls up on a roller; telegraphic message; black valise; papers for BROWN; deeds on parchment with seals.

EXPLANATION OF THE STAGE DIRECTIONS.

The Actor is supposed to face the Audience.

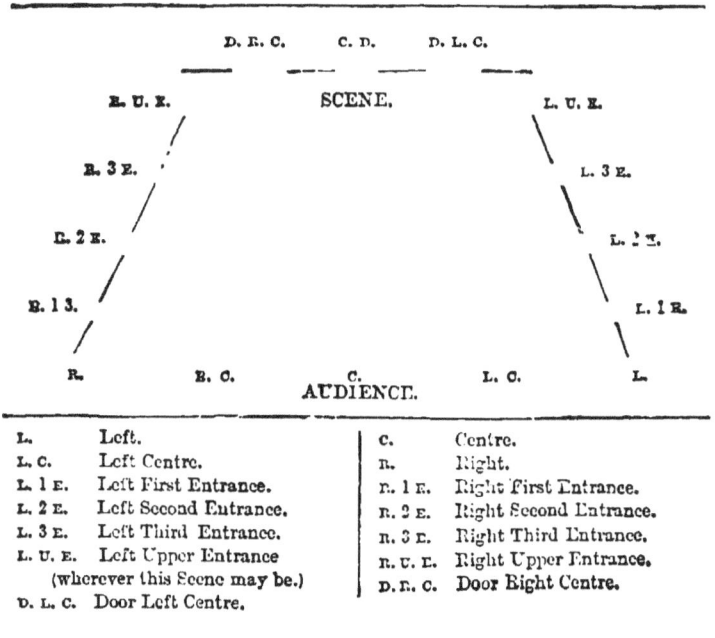

L.	Left.	c.	Centre.
L. C.	Left Centre.	R.	Right.
L. 1 E.	Left First Entrance.	R. 1 E.	Right First Entrance.
L. 2 E.	Left Second Entrance.	R. 2 E.	Right Second Entrance.
L. 3 E.	Left Third Entrance.	R. 3 E.	Right Third Entrance.
L. U. E.	Left Upper Entrance	R. U. E.	Right Upper Entrance.
	(wherever this Scene may be.)	D. R. C.	Door Right Centre.
D. L. C.	Door Left Centre.		

[*For Synopsis see page* 42.]

NEW MEN AND OLD ACRES.

SCENE.—*Room in Cleve Abbey Manor House.*

Discover the BUTLER *arranging books at table,* L. C., *front*

Enter, L. 1 E. D., MRS. BRILL, *the housekeeper.*

MRS. BRILL (*remains* L). Can I say a word to you, sir?

BUTLER (*graciously*). If you can't, Mrs. Brill, who can?

MRS. B. Here's Mr. Secker's* card. (*places card on* L. C. *table*) If Mr. Vavasour is not up, he wishes him to be awakened.

BUT. Quite right.

MRS. B. Indeed. Who's Mr. Secker! (*contemptuously*) He's only an attorney!

BUT. Only an attorney! He's the party that has his finger in every pie in the county, and the licking of it, too! Take care not to offend him, if you like to keep out of hot water. Hush! talking of the Old Gentleman, here he is!

Enter SECKER, L. 1 E. D.

SECKER (*to* MRS. BRILL). Did you tell Mr. Vavasour that I am here?

MRS. B. (*very politely*). He will be told so directly, sir.
[*Exit* L. 1 E. D.

SECK. That's right! (*to* BUTLER) Take my card in—and look sharp! (L. C. *taking one glove off.*) [*Exit* BUTLER, *with card,* R. 1 E. D.

SECK. (*alone*). I don't see how it is to be further delayed. The crash must inevitably come. It's all the result of clients not looking matters in the face. So much the worse for the clients!

Enter, R. 1 E. D., MR. VAVASOUR.

VAVASOUR. Good-morning, Secker! (*shakes hands with* SECKER) I am glad to see you. You were urgent to see me? (*seated* R. *side of table.*)

SECK. (*seated* L. *side of table, a little behind it*). Yes, I wanted you for business, so I come early.

---

* Secker is not a made-up name, as there was an English Archbishop with the same.

Vav. I hope it is not the old story. As a friend, I like to see you every day, but as a lawyer the less often the better.

Seck. (*smiles*). Well, I am afraid that I——

Vav. Afraid?

Seck. Yes. You have run to the end of the tether.

Vav. Ah! What, is the Abbey in danger?

Seck. Yes, you have no means of clearing the mortgage, and the holder insists on having his money.

Vav. He must give more time. He has done it for the last two years.

Seck. That's precisely the reason he won't do so any more. I think he means to force a sale.

Vav (*half rises*). Sell Cleve Abbey! what terrible news for Lady Mildred! Can nothing be done to save us.

Seck. If it is closed now you have a chance of saving some ten thousand from the wreck, but in a year all will be eaten up by the interest.

Vav. It is not for myself—it is for the family and children, and it will be Lilian's first season in London—Lady Mildred has counted *so much* on the result of her appearance.

Seck. You promised to prepare her—and have done so any time these last two years.

Vav. But you do not know what it is to hurt her pride, and I have had to put off the telling her always.

Seck. Very well, but soon, too soon, I fear, she will learn all through a more public medium.

Vav. What! is such utter ruin to come to the head of an ancient family, which returned county members in the reign of Henry the Fourth! Leave the old place to the mercy of strangers. Old houses are like pages in old history, and their associations twine round our hearts like that ivy tapestry upon the ruins of the old Abbey yonder.

Seck. Old families, Mr. Vavasour, are like crops—you exhaust them if you are all the time taking out and never putting in.

Vav. Mr. Secker, I did not expect to hear such revolutionary sentiments from you.

Seck. I am a lawyer, and as such know nothing about revolutions, but we must look facts in the face. What means have you to save your house if the mortgagee stands on his right. You must break it to Lady Mildred. She had far better hear it from you. Besides, I make it my business never to interfere between man and wife. You must face the facts.

Vav. Face the facts! confound it, man, it's how I am to face Lady Mildred. Hush, here she is!

Enter, R. 1 E. D, LADY MILDRED.

Lady Mildred (*with a letter in her hand*). Only think, my dear!—Oh, you, is it, Mr. Secker? (*nods, comes to C.*) I have a letter—and would you believe it, poor Reginald Fitzurse—he has been taken ill with the measles—and he has been only two years married—as if he could not have waited till a more favorable time. (*to* Mr. Vavasour) This will alter the arrangements of Lady Bearholf to take charge of poor Lilian's *debut*.

Vav. And it was so kind of her to take the trouble, quite sisterly—I may even say motherly.

Lady M. Say, motherly—that's the word. She has four daughters of her own, and until she has them all married off to the youngest, do you think she would have let Lilian secure an eligible *parti*. She would not have had a chance. (*goes to* Secker) So, dear Mr. Secker, we must manage the town ourselves. I shall expect you to find me a suitable residence—I prefer Mayfair to Belgravia. We shan't take the horses—so that you must attend to that! (*thoughtfully*) Let me see.

VAV. (*aside to* SECKER). It will be better from you.

SECK. (*aside to* VAVASOUR). Not at all, if it is the place of any one, it is that of yourself.

LADY M. Whispering! Ah! (*threatens them with her forefinger held up, playfully*) If the presence of a lady does not prevent you speaking it underbreath, does it prevent you saying it aloud? (R. C.)

VAV. (C., *hesitating*) The truth is, Mr. Secker has an important matter to impart to your ladyship.

SECK. (L. C.) I beg pardon. It is Mr. Vavasour who wishes your ladyship to understand——

VAV. And so Mr. Secker will explain (*goes up* R. C.)

SEC. It means that the time has come for us to cease—you to spend and I to find means.

VAV. You see, my dear, that Cleve Abbey is threatened with passing into the hands of strangers.

LADY M. Cannot money be raised on the mortgage to pay the interest?

SECK. That has been done so often that it cannot be done again.

LADY M. Is the man so pressing?

SECK. Yes, he wants his money.

LADY M. Can nothing be done?

SECK. Nothing that I can see. In plain English, you have come to the end of the tether. Cleve Abbey sold now, may leave you some consolation, but in a year it will not bring you out clear. (LADY MILDRED *turns to* VAVASOUR.)

VAV. My dear, I endeavored to keep back the crash to the last. I was afraid——

LADY M. Of me? (*smiles*) And I never knew this? (*sadly*) Marmaduke, have I deserved this?

VAV. Have any of us deserved it? I have done all I could. I have gone down on my knees to the fellow, by letter, of course. (R. C.)

LADY M. Anything may be remedied, if taken in time. When the captain gives up the ship the mate must take charge. Trust me, Cleve Abbey may be saved, and without my going on my knees. But we must have time, Mr. Secker. Can't we manage that? We must have no secrets from you, now. Lilian's first season in London must not be compromised, for many reasons. The mortgagee—is he known to you?

SECK. He is an old acquaintance, a man of honor, of wealth, and of position in the mercantile world.

LADY M. Oh, in trade! Ah, then he is open to social influence! We must invite him down.

SECK. He is here!

LADY M. Here?

SECK. Yes, I gave him a card to see the grounds this morning.

VAV. Taking stock, as he calls it! Oh, the callous impudence of these money-grubbers!

LADY M. (*to* VAVASOUR). He is here, and you have not gone to do him the honors. Ask him in. Say Lady Mildred wishes to see him.

VAV. Ah! I smell a rat! Capital idea! capital! Come, Secker, we will try to find him. [*Exit with* SECKER, *French window*, R *in* F.

LADY M. (*alone*). Anything to gain time. Everything depends on that. Our station in the county must be maintained and Lilian's prospects must not be clouded. Let me see. (R C. *front, thoughtfully*.)

Enter, D. *in* L. *of flat,* L. U. E. *corner,* LILIAN.

LILIAN. Ah! so you are there, aunty! (*comes down and kisses* LADY MILDRED.) I suppose you have had breakfast? You really must excuse me for playing truant, but I am floored after the ball last night.

LADY M. Floored! Fatigued, you surely must mean. Now, don't use that dreadful slang.

LIL. But the men like it, mamma!

LADY M. You mistake, my dear! Men may not mind it in showy girls, but they do not like it in fast wives.

LIL. Very well, mamma, only that is not the way my cousin Bertie talks of the times. I've been spending the hour since I was up, in *grinding* him in his English history. Bertie's very weak in history—and I have to reduce it to very small pieces to suit his limited digestion. I'm cramming him, mamma, to pass the Civil Service Examination. I've put the first two lines of French Kings to the tune of Old Rose and Blow the Bellows. (*rattles off a few notes on the piano.*)

LADY M. You must really be less frivolous, Lilian. Come, seriously, how did you enjoy yourself last night?

LIL. Oh, it was awful—(*checks herself*) I mean, it was very jol. There was no end of amusement, though I didn't dance much.

LADY M. With your own set, of course.

LIL. Of course. Stay, I danced twice with a friend of the—(*in a tone of amusement and contempt*) Bunters.

LADY M. You danced with a friend of those odious Bunters, the ludicrous parvenus, who have nothing but their money to support them in the false position into which nothing but their impudence could have intruded them. I thought you would have known better, Lilian. And dance with a friend of theirs! Oh, Lily!

LIL. But he wasn't one of them. A very different kind of man altogether. He was quite thirty—what Bertie calls an old fogy! I only talked with him for sport, and chaffed him frightfully. It was such fun.

LADY M. To you! perhaps not to him.

LIL. Oh, he didn't mind it. Altogether, they are such a game! Old Bunter, with his Methodistical airs and sham piety, and Mother Bunter, (LADY MILDRED *is shocked by all these strong expressions*) with her brags of her old lace and new diamonds. Now Fanny Bunter is not so bad!

LADY M. How you go on! Why, Lilly, every other word you utter is detestable slang. You must learn to speak only as becomes a young lady of your station.

LIL. Oh, mamma, you lecture just like Mr. Brown.

LADY M. Mr. Brown? Brown? I was not aware that we knew anybody of the name of Brown.

LIL. Oh, he's my partner at the ball. (LADY M. *takes seat* L. C., *front, and* LILIAN *sits on footstool at her feet.*)

LADY M. Lilian, the time is come for you to look upon the world with different eyes than a child's. No one can be secure in her happiness beyond the possibility of its loss. Unlike too many mothers, I have never given you a sentimental view of life, but prepared you to look upon marriage as the chief duty and end of your ambition.

LIL. (*carelessly*). Oh, you have told me all that before!

LADY M. Your father is not rich.

LIL. Dear papa, I wish I could fill his dear old pockets.

LADY M. Even young girls may be of assistance in emergencies and alter the direction of affairs. Ah! if I had had such a mother as you, I might have had a very different life.

LIL. (*sharply*). You would not have married papa!

LADY M. (*loftily*). I am not aware that I said anything to warrant such a supposition! Remember, my dear, that in our class, a fortune is the main, nay, indispensable thing. Without it, most things that make life unpleasant, cannot be avoided, and, with it, most things that make life pleasant are to be attained. You must learn to be more circumspect in your actions and your language. Apropos, where do you acquire the blemishes that disfigure your daily speech? (*rises.*)

LIL. (*rises*). Only from my cousin.

LADY M. Detestable slang. By the way you must not be with your cousin Bertie so free and easy.

LIL. Oh, there's no danger there.

LADY M. For you, may be not.

LIL. Pooh, mamma, no man ever fell in love with his coach——

LADY M. Lilian! (*severely.*)

LIL. (*walking up and down with* LADY MILDRED, *who tries to turn away from her*). Now, mamma, that's not slang—it really isn't. It's the regular thing—I mean, it's the correct word —why if Bertie were to come any of his nonsense, I should be down on him like a hammer.

LADY M. Dreadful!

LIL. I beg pardon, I mean, I should shut him up! clap on the extinguisher! (LADY MILDRED *scolds her.*)

Enter, D. *in* F., L. U. E. *corner,* BERTIE FITZURSE.

BER. (*comes down* L., *with book in hand*). I say, Lilly,—oh, I beg pardon, aunty! (L. C. *front*) I say, Lilly, how can you divide 1,781,000 pounds five-and-six-pence, by six-and-eight-pence! Six into one won't go, and eight into five-and-sixpence—I'll be hanged if you can!

LIL. (*comes to* BERTIE). You stupid! you must reduce them both to a common denominator. Excuse me, aunty. (*walks* BERTIE *up* L.) Compound division cuts up poor Bertie badly. Come on, then. Don't you dare argue, sir, with your teacher!

[*Exit, with* BERTIE, D. *in* F., L. U. E. *corner.*

LADY M. The dear child was born to be the leader.

Enter, R. D. *in* F., SECKER *and* BROWN.

SECKER. I beg to present to your ladyship. Mr. Samuel Brown, my friend, and a gentleman of high commercial standing in Liverpool. Brown, Lady Mildred. (*salutations exchanged between* BROWN, *up* R. C., *and* LADY MILDRED, L. C. *front*)

LADY M. You could not have come in more apropos. My daughter and I were just talking of you.

BROWN. Indeed! This morning is full of surprises!

LADY M. She was speaking of the agreeable hour spent at the ball in your company.

BROWN. I should not have guessed it was so agreeable from what impression I had of it.

LADY M. Oh, Lilian is very light, and in the highest of good spirits. That shows how little you men know really of the female heart. I suppose Mr. Vavasour will be happy to show you the farm and the stables, and you must permit me to be your guide over my flower-garden. (*going up* R. C., *with* BROWN, *on his arm*) You know we poor women have to find in them companions—I may almost say friends.

BROWN. At least they have one invaluable quality—they never repeat what they hear.

Lady M. Do you infer that that is why they are always on the blush? This way, Mr. Brown, this way. [*Exit with* Brown, D. F., *and* R. U. E.

Seck. (*by table,* L. C., *alone, aside*). Look after your pockets, Sam Brown. Now, why won't they let such a woman as that step into her husband's shoes, as well as wear his small-clothes? [*Exit,* L. 1 E. D.

Enter, D. F., L. U. *corner,* Bertie, *with a book, and* Lilian. *They come down,* L. C., *to table.*

Bertie. Look here, Lilly! Here's a puzzler for you! (*reads from book*) If twelve dig a trench twenty feet wide, and eight deep and long, in three days of twelve hours, in how many days of nine hours each will it take forty men to dig a trench twenty feet deep, and eight long and wide? How can you do it unless you know how strong the other fellahs are?

Lil. You great stupid! In all such cases the strength is supposed to be equal.

Ber. That won't do! one fellah ain't as strong as another fellah—unless they're twins. You might as well give a fellah the price of beef in the markets and ask him to get up the names, weights, and correct colors of the Derby card.

Lil. Suppose we try it. There, sit you down there! (*they sit at table,* L. C., *front*) Now, will you do the sum, or are you better prepared for your decisive battles.

Ber. (*mournfully*). I know of one decisive battle, and that's between Bertie Fitzurse and his coach. I wonder where you get the patience from to take all this trouble with me.

Lil. It is because I want you to pass with credit.

Ber. But suppose they should put the examination off—they did so once before. Then I should have to be crammed all over again.

Lil. Oh, I'll take care of that. We must get one charge out before we put in another, or the gun would burst!

Ber. (*drawling*). I've almost a mind——

Lil. Doubtful!

Ber. (*quickly*). I've almost a mind to cut the Civil Service, and go out to Australia. A fellah can get a shot there at a kangaroo, or may be go in for an elephant!

Lil. And come back a lion! with a tremendous mane of tawny beard, and a tale—in two volumes! (*laughs.*)

Ber. Ah! you chaff a fellah so! I can't make you out, Lilly! I am very fond of you, not only because you are so good a teacher. You're an awfully jolly girl. And I'd like to ask you a question.

Lil. Oh, anything about the History of England!

Ber. Come, tell me how you like me, not in the way of a coach, but in the way of a lover. (*rises*)

Lil. (*rises*). Now, you be a good boy, Bertie, and don't talk nonsense!

Ber. But I really am in earnest, 'pon my word! A fellah don't like to go down upon his knees, but if that's the correct thing, I will do it.

Lil. No, no! it's anything but the correct thing I assure you. (*walks up and down with* Bertie) Don't you know that it comes under the prohibited degrees, (*with mock solemnity*) A man must not go down on his knees to his coach! No, Bertie! (*with feeling*) you and I are not to think of a union by affection. You are a youth of rank and must look out for a young lady with a fortune, while I—(*aside, tearfully*) I know what I must look out for.

Ber. Money! I don't care a rap for money!

Lil. Bertie! everything is built upon money.

Enter, R.D. 1 F., LADY MILDRED, *remaining up* R. C., *listening, unseen.*

Fortune is the main, nay, the indispensale thing (*imitates the voice of* LADY MILDRED *when she spoke these same words*) to persons in our position of life. Without it most things that make life unpleasant cannot be avoided, but, with it, most things that make life pleasant can be got.

LADY M. (*aside*). My lesson to the letter. (*smiles in satisfaction.*)

BER. Ah, Lillian, I did not think you one of that sort.

LIL D dn't you ?

BER. I didn't believe you would scorn an honest fellah's love, just because he hadn't the hard cash.

LIL. I can't afford. I tell you! But, I tell you what, you behave yourself and I'll coach you in matrimony as well as in mathematics. Why don't you make up to Fanny Bunter?—she's pretty, and she's got lots of money!

BER. If I were to take your advice, I'm sure you wouldn't half like it !

LIL. Just you try ! Don't dare to answer me back ! Am I or am I not your coach, sir ?

BER. The very next time I see Fanny Bunter, I shall make desperate running with her, you shall see if I don't ! [*Exit*, D. F. L. U. *corner.*

LADY M. (*comes down*). Nothing could be better, my dear. (*kisses* LILIAN.)

LIL. Oh, mamma! Were you there ?

LADY M. You have acted very sensibly towards Bertie. But never mind him. There's an acquaintance of yours in the garden, who has been inquiring for you.

LIL. (*goes up* R. C.). Who do you mean, mamma ? (*looks out of* D. F.) Oh, Mr. Brown! P'shaw! I don't care for him.

LADY M. He is a very agreeable gentleman, and I could have wished you had shown him more respect last night.

LIL. Respect to a Mr. Brown! (*mocking* LADY MILDRED'S *voice*) a friend of the Bunters! I was not aware that you were familiar with any person of the name of Brown. (*up* R. C.)

Enter, D. F., VAVASOUR, *with a paper in his hand.*

VAV. A telegram to say that poor Reginald has died of the measles.

LADY M. How dreadful !

VAV. Yes, indeed.

LADY M. Allow me to finish, my dear. How dreadful the disappointment to Lady Fitzurse, she will not be able to bring out her daughters in town this season. By the way, this decease will make a difference in Bertie's prospects.

VAV. Of course, my dear. As the next in the line, failing issue.

LADY M. Ah, perhaps we were wrong to treat him so harshly. (*to* LILIAN.)

LIL. I thought you wanted it, mamma !

LADY M. You will be the best one to tell him of this new.—we are too much affected just now. Break it to him gently.

LIL. Yes, mamma. Only as we have not spoken to Cousin Reginald any time the last five years, I don't see as you can be expected to be much affected. [*Exit*, D. F. L. U. E.

LADY M. (*to* VAVASOUR). Whatever way, Lilian's prospects must not be blighted.

VAV. Ah ! that's just like Reginald ! Always doing things at the wrong time. Now, why could he not have postponed even so urgent a matter to a more convenient moment.

LADY M. Perhaps all is not lost yet. There may still be a way of keeping Cleve Abbey in the family.

VAV. Indeed. How can that be done?

LADY M. Let us marry Lilian to this man who holds the mortgage.

VAV. Ah!

LADY M. He has just told me that Lilian made a peculiar impression upon him.

VAV. Marry Lilian to one of these money-grubbers! Ah! why it is enough to make the Vavasours rise up out of the family vault.

LADY M. Do not give way to sentiment, Marmaduke. There is no other escape. Lilian must sacrifice herself, and what does it matter after all, whether the Abbey descends by the male or female line?

VAV. Better so than not. (sadly) I suppose it is the Law of Nature for these money-grubs to eat up the old trees. But Lilian is the partner for a gentleman, and must not be matched with a snob.

LADY M. Mr. Brown is no snob! He is one of England's Merchant Princes—one of those who have carried and upheld in the most distant lands the character of this little Island.

VAV. Ah! so you have been to the Manchester school?* (talks with LADY MILDRED, R. C.)

Enter, D. F., L. U. *corner*, LILIAN.

LILIAN. That's done. I have told Bertie, mamma. And now, I suppose, we shall all have to doff our fine feathers and put on black?

LADY M. Without delay, my dear.

LIL. And I have got to bid adieu to London in the season—oh, I could cry my eyes out with vexation.

LADY M. It is very disappointing, no doubt, my love, but these things happen under all arrangements.

LIL. But I don't see why, when we didn't care for him while he was alive, we should grieve for him now. It's disgusting hypocrisy to put black on for him when he's gone!

VAV. My dear, you may think so, but you mustn't say so.

LADY M. Family mourning is one of the usages of good society.

LIL. Forgive me, mamma, if I am petulant, but this having to give up the idea of going to London is the ruin of my visions of happiness. I thought, too, that I could then be of service. I love the dear old place, and wanted to save it. We girls are so useless generally that I felt so proud of my chance to do something.

LADY M. Cheer up.

Enter, D. F., R. C., BROWN.

You may do as much here as there, yet.

VAV. Ah, Mr. Brown! I must leave you to the ladies, as I have to write the letters of condolence. (to R. 1 E. D.) Poor Reggy!

[*Exit*, R. 1 E. D.

BROWN (to LILIAN). I must apologize for any faults in my endeavor to entertain you last night.

LIL. No, I am afraid that I annoyed you. (L. C.)

BROWN. It amused you, and it did not hurt me. (C.)

---

* The Manchester school of politicians are those whose platform was planned by Cobden and Bright.

LADY M. (R. C). You have heard of our family bereavement, I believe. Reginald Fitzsure, Lord Bearholm's eldest son, is dead.

BROWN. Yes, Mr. Vavasour said something of the kind. As you had not been on speaking terms with them the last few years I trust the grief is not too heavy to be borne.

LADY M Ah! it is the thought of previous unkindnesses that deepens one's melancholy at moments like these.   [*Exit*, R. 1 E. D.

LILIAN *sits at piano and carelessly plays a fashionable waltz during the following,* BROWN *stands up* R. C. *by the piano.*

LIL. I don't feel as much of it as mamma. I never saw cousin Reginald, so I cannot be expected to be very much grief-stricken, can I ?

BROWN. I should hope not.

LIL. But I am so disappointed not to enjoy the London season.

BROWN. I wonder how you can care for it, living in such a lovely place. Why, I could give up even Liverpool for a home like this.

LIL. Oh, you surely wouldn't compare London with Liverpool !* Liverpool is a smoky, noisy, bustling place, while London is all life, gayety, pleasure !

BROWN. London is well enough in its way, but I am very far of Liverpool, with its bills of lading, dock warrants, invoices —that's the life I have had all my life !

LIL. You must have found it awful dull.

BROWN. Not half so much so as what some people call a life of amusement. Yet I could give up even Liverpool to turn to a quiet life as a gentleman farmer.

LIL. So you are fond of farming, are you ? So am I ! (*getting interested*) Sit down, won't you ? (*goes to* C. *where* BROWN *places chairs for them both, he on her left.*)

BROWN. Thank you.

LIL. Ah! that's hearty! pottering across country on a hundred guinea cob! in all the sports of the county, calling in at every cottage for miles around with kind words to every one and a welcome from all— and then the dear old big-eyed cows, and the dear little calves coming up to rub their cold noses in one's hand.

BROWN. That's young lady farming. I am afraid I should go in for sheep and pigs—a nice lot of plump black Berks, for instance.

LIL. Oh! I like pigs, too! And then there's the county balls, and the schools for the young, and the old women in the alms-houses.

BROWN. I don't know much about old women——

LIL. Altogether there's no life like it. I should like to be a gentleman farmer.

BROWN. That's out of the question. But you may have persuaded me to be one. I think of holding some property in this immediate neighborhood.

LIL. In this county ? Why, there is nothing for sale in this neighborhood at present.

BROWN. But there may be shortly.

LIL. We shall be always glad to hear of you as a neighbor. (*offers her hand.*)

BROWN. Thank you. Ahem ! The Bunters have not found themselves well received here.

LIL. Oh, the Bunters! They thought their money would open all the

---

* The Liverpudlians speak of London as the Bostonians or Philadelphians of New York.

doors in the county, and so it was a pleasure to shut them in their faces. Come, you must acknowledge that Bunter is an unmistakable cad! (BROWN *starts in surprise*) As for his wife, whatever she puts on, she is a guy! a downright corkscrew! At least, that's what Bertie calls her. Bertie is my cousin—he's staying down here with us, studying for the Civil Service examination. I am coaching him in English History.

BROWN. And he is teaching you the English language!

LIL. What! have I said anything a little too strong?

BROWN. You must admit that "cad" is a rather strong expression in a young lady's mouth.

LIL. (*half offended*). Oh, I like words that there can't be any mistake about!

BROWN. I should think there was some mistake about "cad" and "guy," and such like.

LIL. We old families are not like such vulgar *parvenus*. Say what they will, there are some things which cannot be bought with money.

BROWN. Can you tell me what they are?

LIL. The honor and credit of an old name, the pride of a long line of noble ancestry, that makes the least of us equal to the highest of the unknown.

BROWN. Oh, I grant you, the past is yours. But the future belongs to the new men with brains to think out a way, and hands to make it, and not to those who sit in a corner with their hands folded because their forefathers did something or other before they were born.

LIL. Well, the future can't belong to people like the Bunters, who don't know who was their grandfather—or it wouldn't be a future at all.

BROWN (*rises*). I don't know my grandfather. He is merged into the vast congregation of the Browns. But still it is a consolation to know that one must have had a grandfather some time.

LIL. Ah! you cannot be expected to understand these things as we old families look upon them. (*rises.*)

Enter LADY MILDRED, R. 1 E. D.

LADY M. Well, Mr. Brown, have you made your peace with the young lady?

BROWN. I was not aware of any cause of enmity between us, and if so I trust that has been dissipated by our conversation. (*gives* LADY MILDRED *his arm and they exeunt*, R. D. F.)

LIL. (*alone by table*, L. C.). I don't like him a bit. What right has he to correct my English? I wonder what makes mamma so civil to him?

Enter SERVANT, L. 1 E. D.

SERVANT. Mr. and Mrs. Bunter, Miss Bunter and Mr. Blazenbaig.

LIL. (*aside*). The Bunters! Oh, mamma wouldn't see them for the world. (*aloud*) Tell them we are out. Ah, too late!

Enter, L. 1 E. D., MR. BUNTER, MRS. BUNTER, FANNY BUNTER, *and* BLAZENBAIG. *Exit* SERVANT.

MRS. BUNTER. My dear Miss Vavasour! We beg to return your fan which you left last night in our carriage. (*gives fan to* LILIAN.)*

LIL. Thank you. (*puts fan* R., *on table or stand.*)

---

* LILIAN.	MRS. BUNTER.	BUNTER.	FANNY.	BLAZENBAIG.
R. C.	C		L. C.	L.

Mrs. B. The day was so fine that we thought we would call and return it.

Bunter. And wherever I call, I make it a p'int to walk in.

Blaz. Ah, mine frien' Bunter, he make it a p'int to valk into efervbody vat he calls on.

Bun. This is Professor Blazenbaig. I call him my Chancellor of the Exchequer, my Commissioner of Works! (*slaps* Blazenbaig *on the shoulder.*)

Blaz. Nefer you mind vat mine frien' Bunter say! He is komisch—vat you call, a vag—yah, a vag! a man mit a strong feeling for de humor! (*to* Bunter, *aside*) I vants to shpy about. I vill regonnoitre der groundt. (*goes up to* R. D. F)

Lil. I must make excuses in case you should not see mamma. She is much distressed with the news of the death in Lord Bearholme's family, the elder brother of my cou in Bertie Fitzurse.

Mrs. B. The *Honorable* Bertie Fitzurse! What a dreadful affliction! Pray convey to your mother the expression of how much we feel for her.

Bun. (*like a stump-preacher*). Thus we are cut down like a flower! What are rank and titles which do not cling to a man, while native nobility never deserts us. When I came to the great metropolis I had only three pence in coppers in my pocket! and not a friend in the world! but I had h'industry and h'energy, and with h'industry *and* h'energy I rose to the proud position of the humble individual you see before you.

Mrs. B. (*angrily*). I don't see what cause you have to go backward like that.

Bun. (*taking a step forward*). Because I have come forward like this! And besides we read that it is not good to be puff-ed up!

Mrs. B. (*looks up stage to* Lilian). What a pleasant view you have from here. I declare you have quite a h'ornament in the deerpark and the Abbey Ruins.

Fanny (*sentimentally*). Oh, how delightful! I adore ruins! They speak to me with the voices of ages. Hark! I can hear them now! Don't you hear them now?

Lil. (*smiles*). No! that is only something in the wind.

Mrs. B. I like ruins, too. If I had my way I should have had Beaumanor Park laid out in ruins, but Bunter has some objections.

Bun. Not for the expense. But to you old families, old furniture, old ruins, old antiquities and to us modern h'elegance and h'opulence like ours!

Lil. (*aside*). Why won't they go? (*impatiently.*)

Mrs. B. While I am here, I should so like to see your greeneries and glasses.

Bun. And iron, my dear! Glass *and* iron are the two main supports of our age, and, with the hot water pipes no progress is impossible under modern civilization. (*to* Lilian) I have three acres of land under glass in cultivation, and my pineries are equal to Chatsworth. At least, my gardener says so, and I pay him enough for him to ought to know! But what is man that he should boast, for he is but a flower—here to-day and gone to-morrow!

Lil. The gardener will show you around. (*to* R. 1 E. D., *aside*) For what I have escaped, may I be truly thankful to my stars.

[*Exit*, R. 1 E. D.

Fan. (*admiring cabinet*). Oh, papa! mamma! come and see this beautiful buhl! (*up* R C.)

Bun. What's that? a beautiful bull? you mean that little cow out there on the lawn?

Fan. No, papa, I meant this buhl. B-u-h-l, buhl.

Bun. (*shakes his head gravely*). No, my dear! there may be many modern h'innovations, and many foreign fashions introduced but b-u-double-l spells bull all the world over!

Fan. Oh, there's no use speaking to papa. (*to* Mrs. Bunter, *who is looking at photographic album on table up* l. c.) Only look at this marque-try, mamma.

Bun. Well, this is the first time I ever knew you to take an interest in marketry! (Fanny *tosses her head indignantly, and converses with* Mrs. Bunter.)

Enter, r. d. f., Blazenbais, *excited. Comes down to* Bunter, c.

Blaz. Hurrah! mein frien'! It's all right! Sooch magnificent kidneys! der groundt is full mit de hematite! Dere is tousands und tousands in der mines oonder below our foot!

Bun. (*delighted*). Then we will have those kidneys in our pockets! (*rubs his hands*) Mind that nobody here gets an inkling of the secret.

Blaz. Goot! I vas oop to a snuff!

Bun. Brown is over here. Do you think he knows anything?

Blaz. Dere is no fear, I haf sounded Brown. He knows nothing. (*converses animatedly with* Bunter, l. c. *front*.)

Mrs. B. (*comes down* c., *small album open in her hand*). Oh, look here! if it isn't Mr. Bertie Fitzurse!

Fan. So it is! my partner at the ball last night.

Mrs. B. Such a very h'elegant young man.

Bun. Banks his money at the Bank of Elegance!*

Mrs. B. (*suddenly*). Lord Bearholme's eldest son having died, this Mr. Fitzurse may be a lord some day.

Fan. Dear me! I thought there was something *distingué* about him. He waltzed so divinely!

Bun. We should be thankful we are not members of a bloated aristocracy! How can they expect to prosper when they know not the principles of piety and business?

Fan. What dreadful sentiments, papa!

Bun. All that is great and profitable in civilization comes out of the brains and bank books of the middle-class.

Mrs. B. But where will you find such intelligence and refinement as in the nobles of England?

Enter, l. d. f., Bertie, *coming down* l. *with paper and pencil in his hands.*

Ber. I say, Lilly, how do you spell sympathy? with a y or with an i? (*looks up confused*) I—I beg your pardon. I didn't know that anybody was here. (*to* Fanny) How daw yah do? You haven't seen any one yet? Can I be of any service to yaw?

Mrs. B. Miss Vavasour has only just left us. We were waiting for the gardener to show us the flowers.

Ber. (*puts away pencil and paper eagerly*). Can't I have the pleasyar? I assure yaw, most happy—I have positively nothing to do. (c. *front*.)

Enter, r. 1 e. d., Lilian.

Lil. What's that I hear, sir? nothing to do! (r. c. *front*.)

---

* "Bank of Elegance" bills are similar to the valentines printed as cards on the "Bank of Love," and sometimes used by counterfeiters.

BUN. Well, Blazenbaig, we'll take a walk around the Home Farm. You won't mind us running away, ladies? Come along, Blazenbaig.

[*Exit*, L. 1 E. D., *with* BLAZENBAIG, *talking with him.*

FAN. (R. C. *with* BERTIE). Are you fond of flowers, Mr. Fitzurse?

BER. They're very pretty, but they are rayther dear for the button-hole.

FAN. Oh, I adore flowers! Do you not think they have a life of their own—a speech? I can find a voice even in a hedge.

BER. Ya-as, a fellah is never lonely with a *weed*.

FAN. And then their perfume! Don't you admire flowers for their perfume?

BER. Never could bear them, even in the open air.

FAN. Do you remember what Wordsworth says: "A yellow primrose by the river's brim, was but a primrose—nothing more to him."

BER. "Nothing more to him." I wonder what more could it be? (*gives his arm to* FANNY, *and they exeunt*, R. D. F.)

MRS. B. Oh! I declare! there's Mr. Fitzurse and Fanny walking off together *tater-tater!* (*up* R. C.) Dear me! and there's your mamma in the garden, arm in arm with Mr. Brown! I knew your papa was in difficulties, but I should have thought Mr. Brown a man of more taste than to intrude himself here.

LIL. What do you mean? I don't understand. (*puzzled*) Why should not Mr. Brown call on us here. You introduced him to me at the ball last night.

MRS. B. Why, everybody knows. Your papa has mortgaged his estate, and he does not find it easy to pay—and that's why he thinks it just as well to be kind to the mortgagee, who is Mr. Brown.

LIL. My papa owes Mr. Brown money, and cannot pay. (*seated at* L. C. *table.*)

MRS. B. And he is going to force a sale. (*seated at* L. C. *table.*)

LIL. Sell Cleve Abbey!

MRS. B. Brown is not such a fool as to lose the property, unless your mamma talks him over. And there's nothing a woman can't do with her speech. You ought to see the cheques I have swindled Bunter out of.

LIL. You surely must be mistaken.

MRS. B. Indeed, I am not mistaken. The whole county talks of it, but you may easily never have heard of it. But such things are all the time happening. I dare say there will be a good sum if the estate is sold now. (*going up* C.) Perhaps Bunter may make a bid for it. I don't dislike the place, come to look at it. [*Exit*, R. D. F.

LIL. (*standing, leaning one hand on table, in painful thought*). This explains why mamma was so kind to him. Can it be that strangers may yet live in Cleve Abbey? Sell the dear old place! Oh! poor papa! (*hand to her eyes.*)

Enter, R, D. F., BROWN, *hat in hand.*

BROWN (*cheerily*). Your mother insists upon it that we are not yet good friends. (*comes down* C.) I have come to do away with that impression before I say good-morning. You turn away your head. Why do you look so pale? Can your mother have been right?

LIL. (*tearfully*). When you said that you meant to buy an estate in this neighborhood this morning, I did not know what I know now. It was Cleve Abbey! (BROWN *starts in surprise, he puts his hat on table*) You hold a mortgage on it, and my papa will be forced to sell the Abbey.

BROWN (*gravely*). I do not think that is a proper subject to be discussed between us.

LIL. (*sadly*). Ah! you think me a mere girl, like the rest of them.

BROWN. No!

LIL. Thank you for that. Is it true my papa will be forced to sell our home?

BROWN. I am afraid—your father's embarrassment is deep——

LIL. I understand—I understand. We must leave the roof that has been over those of our name so long. If they sell the Abbey, you mean to buy.

BROWN. Well, really, I—I would rather you would not press me.

LIL. Somebody, I suppose, must buy it.

BROWN. If I do, is there anything you would like me to do?

LIL. I hope you will keep up the old place? (BROWN *nods*) The house and the garden—and the sundial with the broken nose—(*suppresses her tears*) and the fish-pond—there are no fish in it now, and it is full of duckweed, but I shouldn't like to hear of it's being removed.

BROWN. The fish shall be religiously kept out and the duckweed as religiously kept in—I assure you. I shall do everything you wish.

LIL. Then there's the school——

BROWN. Oh, that's to my taste—I will have it put in thorough repair, and see the teachers have vigorous young blood.

LIL. No, no! you must keep the old masters!

BROWN. Are they up to the mark?

LIL. I don't know. I only know they have been there ever since I can remember. Then there's the old women in the Vavasour Almshouses. How they will miss me on Wednesdays!

BROWN. I fear I cannot make up for you in that.

LIL. (*half smiling*). Tea and tobacco will go a great way towards that.

BROWN. I promise.

LIL. Bless you! (*takes* BROWN'S *hand*) Then there's my old thorough-bred mare—she's past moving now; and Nep, my black retriever—and the lame peacock with one eye—I think you will do all you promise.

BROWN. Thank you. (*shakes her hand*) Is there anything more?

LIL. No. Thank you so much—thank you! (*with an effort*) Good-morning!

BROWN. Good-morning, Miss Vavasour! (*their hands reluctantly let go, and* BROWN *goes a little up* C.)

LIL. (*bursts into sobbing*). Oh! I can't bear it!

BROWN (*turns and comes beside her*). Oh, Miss Vavasour, why do you expose yourself and me to this pain.

Enter, R. D. F., LADY MILDRED, *who remains up* C., *looking at the speakers in surprise and then in pleasure.*

Pray compose yourself! I wish I could tell you how much I feel for you (*takes her hand and supports her*) and yours. (LILIAN *is about to cling to him, half fainting.*)

PICTURE.

LADY MILDRED (*up* C

BROWN *and* LILIAN (C. *front.*)

SLOW CURTAIN.

ACT II.

SCENE.—*Abbey Ruins in 5th grooves. Afternoon.*

Discover FANNY *and* BERTIE, *playing croquet*, R. C.

FAN. (*drives ball through hoop*). One for me. (*sings*) I'm afloat! I'm afloat! etc. (BERTIE *takes a seat on settee* R. *front, and fans himself as if fatigued*) It's no use giving you grace—you have no chance in the game.

BER. Ya-as, there's no use my sticking up to play it—unless you will coach me in croquet as Lilly has in the history. Ah! that examination was an awful hard thing! You don't mind a cigarette, do you?

FAN. No! (*playing with croquet mallet and the balls.*)

BER. By Jove! A fellah wants a deal of rest after so much exertion. I really enjoy the quiet life we lead down here.

Enter, R. U. E , LILIAN.

LIL. (*comes down* c.). Poor thing! If there had been any more of it, you couldn't have pulled through. You may be suffering from paralysis of the brain. It's very dangerous.

BER. By Jove! I hope I shall get over it. Rather hard for a fellah after he has won a place not to be able to do the work of it

FAN. You can leave it to Miss Vavasour—she will continue to coach you.

LIL. (*mallet in hand*). My name is Lilian, just as your is Fanny, and if you call me Miss Vavasour again, I will croquet you into the middle of next week! Is no one going to play now? I must look for a pupil. Oh here comes Mr. Brown!

Enter BROWN, R. U. E.

BROWN (*comes down and gently refuses to have the mallet offered him by* FANNY). Thank you, I do not understand even the alphabet of croquet.

LIL. Bertie has passed the examination, and now he is awaiting the result with confidence. I hope all my efforts with him won't end in smoke. That would be hard on me as his master. Now, I didn't say "coach" that time.

FAN. I shall be off for home soon, and before I leave I should like a last look around.

BER. (*rises lazily*). If you like I'll go with you, though there's nothing I care to look at save yourself.

LIL. Don't leave him, Fanny! In his anxiety, he is not safe left alone. (*laughs.*)   [*Exeunt* FANNY *and* BERTIE, L. U. E.

BROWN (*to* LILIAN). I too am going to-day.

LIL. Going away?

BROWN. I must. My time here has passed like a dream.

LIL. Can you not stay longer?

SERVANT *enters* L. 2 E , *and removes croquet.*

BROWN. I am afraid not. It depends on circumstances.

LIL. (*archly*). Am *I* one of the circumstances?

BROWN. There is business to be done which I cannot manage down here.

LIL. So you *must* go?

BROWN. Yes. You see, there is a prospect of what we call dirty weather on 'Change. My firm is not mixed up with rash speculations, but all manner of ships are shattered in a storm, and it is the duty of the captain to be on deck with the rest at the first whistle of the tempest.

LIL. And we have detained you here when your presence was needed t'iere.

BROWN. You see I must leave you.

LIL. I should do the same if I were a man. (*looks up* L.) Oh! there's that foreign gentleman, Mr. Blazenbaig.

BROWN. Fishing!

LIL. Yes. I wish papa had not given him leave. He is always fishing, but he never catches anything.

BROWN (*aside*). I suspect what he is after. (*aloud*) There he goes. He pretends not to see us.

LIL. But he shan't escape. (*raises her voice*) Here, Mr. Blazenbaig!

BROWN (*loudly*). Mr. Blazenbaig! (*in usual voice*) He looks like a cat caught stealing cream.

Enter, L. U. E., BLAZENBAIG, *with fishing-pole and basket.*

BLAZENBAIG. Goot-morning, Miss Fafasauer! goot-morning, Prown! (*salutes.*)

LIL. Have you had much sport? What have you caught? (BLAZENBAIG *tries to avoid her.*)

BROWN. Ah! you have been spearing, I see? (*points to spike at end of fishing-pole.*)

BLAZ. (*laughs*). Yah, yah! dat ish a schpear of mine own invention—I stick him in der groundt und wait for a bite.

LIL. I never see you with any fish. Is that for ground bait?

BLAZ. (*laughs*). Groundt bait! Yah, das is it! it vas vor groundt bait, yah! Ha, ha!

LIL. Let's have a look at your haul. (BLAIZENBAIG *tries to evade her*) There's a tax on minnows. Nothing under half a pound goes free.

BLAZ. (*resisting*). They are too schmall to be looked at! (LILIAN *seizes basket playfully*) Himmel! I must go in der drain!

LIL. Go into what drain?

BLAZ. I must go to town! in der railway dra'n!

BROWN. Oh! (*takes basket from* LILIAN) Hullo! it is very heavy for small fish. (LILIAN *holds* BLAZENBAIG *back*) I wonder what is in it? (*turns contents of basket out.*)

LIL. (*stoops over basket*). Only weeds and stones! not even a tittlebat!

BROWN (*gravely*). There, Mr. Blazenbaig! (*returns basket, but absently retains one or two of the pebbles*) I didn't know you were a geologist?

BLAZ. (*fills the basket as before*). A leedel, Prown, I vas look for de flints und kelts of der pre-hisdoric dimes—der weapons of der beeple before der worldt!

BROWN (*looking at stones*). Well, the people that used such things for weapons must have been very much behind the world! I should think.

BLAZ. Ach! we Germans are more gifen to study und not so mooch to der money-getting, to der goldt, as you Englanders are.

LIL. Wasting your time on stones, not even precious stones! Rubbish!

BROWN. Ah! time and stones have more value than some people are aware of.

BLAZ (*suspiciously*). Vat do you mean, Prown?

BROWN. Oh, nothing! (*pockets the pebbles he picked up*) Time after brings forth the value of stones even.

Blaz. (*aside*). I haf blind them—the secret is safe—and I half der tousands! Now for der drain!   [*Exit*, R. 1 E.

Lil. Poor man! the idea of getting so excited about specimens of the ground here.

Brown. The poor man of to-day may be the rich man of to-morrow. Don't laugh at those who do anything foolish if they have good grounds to go on.

Enter, L. 1 E., Lady Mildred, *with a shawl wound round her shoulders.*

Lady M. Good news! (*waves a large envelope*) Bertie has passed with flying colors!

Lil. Oh, I am so glad. (*takes the envelope and looks at letter within.*)

Brown (*to* Lilian). I congratulate you on the success of your pupil.

Lady M. Ah! no one knows how much he owes to Lilian's pains and patience.

Lil. Never mind, mamma. All I have done will be repaid by one favor I ask of you.

Lady M. What's that?

Lil. Let me carry him the news.

Brown. In the days of my father, I have heard him say the *coach* that bore tidings of a victory had its wheels bound with laurels.

Lil. Good-by, mamma! (*sings*) "See the conquering hero comes!" (*runs off* L. U. E.)

Lady M. So lighthearted! And she is always most happy in making others so.

Brown. An admirable trait.

Lady M. She will make an inestimable companion to the man who can appreciate her.

Brown. That brings me to a subject of conversation which I wished to broach—I have—that is—I beg your pardon, it is not very easy to express what I want to say. Won't you sit down? (*brings chairs to C. front and they take seats*) This may be the last time I see you, for I leave here to-day.

Lady M. That is much too short a time.

Brown. Before I go, let me thank you for the pleasure you have given me in my stay.

Lady M. Mutual, my dear sir. And your delicate kindness in one important matter puts us under great obligations to you.

Brown. There is a way of putting me in your debt!

Lady M. Indeed! how is it?

Brown. By letting it depend on her and me alone that your daughter should be my wife.

Lady M. Lilian your wife!

Brown. Yes.

Lady M. It is so unexpected! you have taken me quite by surprise.

Brown. Yet I do not think that it is too rash of me. I fancy I have some good reasons to make the offer.

Lady M. One moment. Have you spoken to Lilian?

Brown. Not yet; but in such matters, a man may express a good deal without speaking.

Lady M. (*sentimentally*). Lilian is so much what I was at her age—so innocent of the harsh realities of this world—all feeling.

Brown. I think I can see all the disparities of our positions—your daughter Lilian is a lady of high rank, in all the bloom of youth, while I am a sedate man of thirty-three. Rank and youth are desirable qualities in their way, but on the other hand—(*hesitates*) really, I don't know whether I ought to go on in this strain.

LADY M. Nothing could be more natural and straightforward——

BROWN. I have certain social advantages—and I can give the woman of my choice the whole of a loving heart——

LADY M. I can perfectly believe it.

BROWN. I should like you to look at the matter from a purely business point of view.

LADY M. My dear sir! What mother could look at her daughter's marriage from a business point of view?

BROWN. Impossible! But supposing you could, I should wish your attention. The net profits of my firm are some fifteen thousand a year, and the name of Brown & Co. stands as high as any other house. I have my ambition, and what I hope to attain alone, I ought to accomplish all the sooner for having an inestimable wife by my side. As for the mortgage I hold on the Abbey, I should consider that as an outside matter altogether, not to be spoken of between us; and effectually to remove it, I should make it over to my wife on the wedding day. Come, I don't think you can object to me, even from the business point of view.

LADY. You call this looking at it from a business point of view?

BROWN. What do you call it?

LADY M. (*rises*). The most generous and noble proposition that ever emanated from the heart of man.

BROWN. Then I have your consent? (*puts away the chairs.*)

LADY M. (*gives her hand*). And my best wishes. Mr. Vavasour may entertain objections, founded on his repugnance to any person connected with mercantile pursuits, but I don't think there will be any difficulties there that I cannot remove.

BROWN. Thanks.

LADY M. You say you are ambitious. Then there's no reason you should remain as you are. Have you never thought of getting into Parliament?

BROWN. Is there any man with a head on his shoulders who has not had that desire?

LADY M. Yes, the House is accessible to most ambitious men nowadays. I think we could return you from here for about two thousand pounds. There is a Purity of Elections Party in the town, and so it could not be done for less.

BROWN. Much obliged.

LADY M. Once in the House, your advance will be rapid and unimpeded. Of course you will only speak on questions of trade and commerce.

BROWN. Well, that does not come up to my idea of a member's duties.

LADY M. That will get you talked about in the papers, and we will manage with our family influence to secure you the first vacancy—something in the Board of Trade—these are always promising some new man with novel ideas.

BROWN. The coming man who never comes.

LADY M. Lilian will be admirable to preside over your house—there's nothing like a lady to carry out the mining into the social division of the enemy, and of course you will have a house for London in the season, in a fashionable quarter. I will manage that for you!

BROWN. Are you not promising too much?

LADY M. Dear, no! I never take more upon my shoulders than I am able to support.   [*Exit*, L. 2 E.

Enter LILIAN, *gayly*, L. U. E.

LIL. There! I have made Bertie happy, and Fanny too. Do you know, I think they will make a match of it? I am so glad for Bertie's sake.

BROWN. You are thinking more of them than they are of you. People in love never have a thought of others.

LIL. That is not my idea of love—I think it the most unselfish of passions. If I were in love, I believe my greatest happiness would be in making others happy.

BROWN. What you say emboldens me. I have something to tell you before I go away. (*places chair for* LILIAN *and stands beside her*) Lilian—I beg pardon, Miss Vavasour.

LIL. I like Lilian best!

BROWN. Lilian, be it. I am going away to-day, you know.

LIL. Your stay away won't be long, I hope.

BROWN. It will be for longer than I wish, if you do not prevent that.

LIL. *I* may let you stay here. How can that be?

BROWN. I wish to tell you a serious thing—the most serious thing that a man can say in his life. I love you, Lilian! (*her business of surprise, pleasure, coyness, etc.*) You turn away! Tell me I have no hope and put me out of my misery.

LIL. (*archly*). Is it such misery?

BROWN. Do you mean that you can love me?

LIL. You make me very proud and happy!

BROWN. (*under his breath joyfully*). Proud and happy! (*takes her hand*) Don't jest with me. No, you are kind and good. You see in me a man of years, whose capital of love has not been wasted in the small change of flirtations. I love you, I love you much more than I can ever say, and I shall do my best that your path in life shall be without a care.

LIL. I am sure of it.

BROWN. You will be my wife?

LIL. What more could I hope to be?

BROWN. My own! (*kisses her hands.*)

LIL. (*delighted*). Oh! (*pause*) Now, tell me, when did you first begin to fall in love with me?

BROWN. The day I first saw you.

LIL. You darling! (*kisses* BROWN.)

BROWN. When I came down to see the property—(LILIAN *looks playfully offended*) I don't mean you! and I heard you speak so sweetly of the old places, the sundial and the lame peacock—and when you broke down altogether, through your tears you showed me your heart and its worth.

· LIL. I tried hard to keep them down, but I am glad I cried, now. Have you spoken to mamma?

BROWN. Yes, and she has given her consent. And she has not only promised to speak to your father, but she has already planned out our future. We are to live in town, and I am to be made a sort of imitation nobleman and sit in Parliament.

LIL. I like you as you are best.

BROWN. I prefer to see my name at the tail of the Liverpool 'Change list than at the head of the column of fashionable intelligence in the *Morning Post*.

LIL. (*smiling*). John Bull's Paradise; or, the Snobs' Elysium, as I call it.

BROWN. It is rather late in life for a man to dance attendance in a court suit, who has grown gray in mercantile strife.

Lil. I want to know no other world than yours.

Brown. I must warn you—you will have a rival.

Lil. A rival?

Brown. Yes, the office! even while I love you, I shall still stick to business.

Lil. Shall I *try* to win you away from that? I am not afraid but that I shall become all you wish of me. (*rises*)

Brown. My dear Lilian! (*rises, they walk up and down during following*) But there will be time enough for grave matters. Meanwhile, let us bask in the sun of love and happiness, uninterrupted by a single thought. (*change of tone to ordinary one*) There's some one coming.

Lil. (*looks up* L., *vexed*). It is Bertie and Fanny.

Brown. On the most affectionate terms it would appear.

Lil. How disgusting it is for people to be spoons, isn't it, dear?
[*Exit with* Brown, *very lovingly,* L. 1 E.

Enter, L. U. E., Bertie *and* Fanny, *coming down* C.

Ber. I wish that I had tried for the F. O.'s.

Fan. What's the F. O.?

Ber. The Foreign Office. Awful swells—come at one, go at four! invited everywhere, up to everything—but it is deuced expensive—all your money goes for gloves and *eau de cologne*—so that there's no use of my thinking of it. I would like to be one of those other fellahs.

Fan. What other fellows?

Ber. The fellahs in the city, who look after the what's its names—the gray shirtings. "Cochineals are dull, and gray shirtings lively."

Fan. I don't care for cochineals, and as for gray shirtings, I don't even know what they are. (*front.*)

Ber. (*front*). It must be rather hard on a fellah to have to record that "money is tight." I have found that money is always tight.

Fan. I detest money.

Ber. Do you, now?

Fan. Yes, I have seen so much of it.

Ber. I have not. I suppose that makes the difference.

Fan. It causes so much misery.

Ber. It has often made me feel that.

Fan. Money is but dross. How much higher than the ore of gold, the love of art as exemplified in the Stones of Venice. I could live on Ruskin.

Ber. Could you? That would come cheaper than the co-operative stores. I say, Fanny—I beg your pardon—does it matter if I call you Fanny?

Fan. (*sentimentally*). Oh, no.

Ber. Look here, Fanny. If a fellah with only ninety a year was to ask you if you thought you could marry him—what would you say?

Fan. Oh, what an idea!

Ber. If I were to say so?

Fan. Oh, Mr. Fitzurse!

Ber. Say Bertie!

Fan. (*affectedly*). Oh, Ber-tie!

Ber. And that means "yes!"

Fan. Ye-es.

Ber. There's no one looking! Couldn't you give a fellow a kiss? (*embraces* Fanny) That's awful jolly! I say, do you think your father will give his consent?

Fan. I could coax him, and I think he would.

BER. Tell him that it's awful difficult to pass the Civil Service examination; it takes no end of brains—and all that. And you might put it to him that I may be a lord some day.

FAN. A real lord. In the House—a great Radical? Papa will be pleased to think of that. Dear me, if this had only happened sooner.

BER. What for?

FAN. I have got to go home to-day.

BER. But I can see you elsewhere.

FAN. So you can. Won't you do me a favor? Pluck me one little modest flower.

BER. A flower? (*goes* R.) Tame or wild?

FAN. Wild.

BER. (*gets flower*). A dandelion! will that do.

FAN. Yes. I will place it on my heart, as a sweet *souvenir* of the time—the place——

BER. And the party! eh, Fanny?

FAN. Oh, my beloved! (*they embrace affectedly.*)

BER. Oh, my—give me another kiss, Fanny! [*They exeunt,* R. 1 E.

Enter, L. 2 E., LADY MILDRED *and* VAVASOUR.

LADY M. (*eye-glass up*). Isn't that Bertie and Fanny.

VAV. Yes. By Jove, Bertie's arm is round her waist. And there, by George, he has kissed her.

LADY M. Twice! (*laughs*) Come, Marmaduke, I don't think it hardly fair to watch them.

VAV. I don't see that I should let them bill and coo under the trees in her father's absence, while Fanny is entrusted to us.

LADY M. Don't be alarmed. I arrange t it all. I meant her to be a foil to Lilian, and come between her and Bertie. Lilian's prospects must not be weakened.

VAV. I see—Lilian and Brown, rank and money—Fanny and Bertie, money and rank. Well, well, you know best, my dear.

LADY M. In a few things, I do;—marriage is one of them.

VAV. I will swallow the black draught—I should say, the brown one—but don't ask me to *like* it!

LADY M. While you give your blessing, your private opinion does not so much matter.

Enter, L. 2 E., SECKER, *with a handful of letters in envelopes, unsealed.*

Ah, Mr. Secker.

SECK. (*salutes*). I want Mr. Brown. Is he not here? These letters are for him. (*gives letters to* VAVASOUR.)

VAV. (*looks at letters*). "Important and Immediate." And they are three days old!

SECK. The lad in my office was too stupid to forward them.

LADY M. Mr. Secker, I ask you to congratulate us.

SECK. I do congratulate you. Pray, what for?

LADY M. Mr. Brown has proposed to Lilian.

SECK. (*aside*). Hooked him, by Jove!

LADY M. Lilian was much prepossessed by him on their first interview, and his stay rapidly advanced him in her good opinion. It is quite a love match. (*c.*)

VAV. According to what my lady says, Mr. Brown is a man of first-rate abilities.

LADY M. And great talents.

Vav. And considerable money. (R. C.)

Seck. (L. C.). I don't know of a man of more worth or worth more—he comes out right both ways. I congratulate you on him, and him on securing an excellent wife.

Vav. And an inestimable mother-in-law. (*goes up with* Secker, *in conversation, and they exeunt* R. U. E)

Lady M. (*aside*). With the assurance that Cleve Abbey is safe from such people, I can meet them with patience.

Enter, L. 2 E., Bunter, Mrs. Bunter *and* Blazenbaig, *the latter remaining* L.

Lady M. I am glad to see you. (*shakes hands with* Mrs. Bunter.)

Mrs. B. We have come for Fanny, and we hope you are pleased with her.

Lady M. Yes, she has become a fast friend of Lilian's, and we shall always see her with pleasure.

Bun. (*showing his watch*). Punctuality, my lady, is the soul of business. Fanny is due home at four-thirty, and the time's up.

Enter, L. 2 E., Telegraph Messenger, Blazenbaig *takes telegram from him.*

Bun. What's that? (Mrs. Bunter *and* Lady Mildred *converse up* R. C.)

Blaz. (*to* Bunter). A delegram.

Bun. Ah! that's the wust of being a public man—these things are always following you about. An invitation to some dinner, or to lay the corner-stone of some chapel. (*gives telegram to* Blazenbaig, *for him to open it*) Well, what are you waiting for? (*to* Messenger)

Mess. I have another for Mr. Brown.

Lady M. I am going to him. You can follow me. (Messenger *goes up* R. C.; *to wait.*)

Mrs. B. (*to* Lady Mildred). How lovely this place is close to. As I have said to Bunter, really I must have our place laid out in ruins like these.

Bun. And as I have always said to you, Maria, my dear, don't be ridiculous!

Lady M. Ah! there are some things that money cannot buy—the memories round old places, the history of old pictures, the glories like these upon this ground. Plant money, and it never will take root—plant a race like ours, and it lasts beyond the present day. (*to* Mrs. Bunter) Come, my dear.

[*Exeunt* Lady Mildred, Mrs. Bunter *and* Messenger, R. U. E.

Bun. (*aside*). I don't like that woman! Sometimes I think she is insulting me, and sometimes that she is humbugging me. (*aloud*) Well, Blazy, my boy, what is it?

Blaz. (*reading telegram*). Hundertausendpoppelgeists!

Bun. Eh? That's profane swearing, though in the German language. Don't do it again! for I can't abide with profanity, though in a foreign tongue—it hurts my feelings. (C. *front*)

Blaz. (L. C. *front*). I vas schwear for mine luck, und you will schwear also for your goot fortune luck when you shall hear. Great failure in the city. The Imperial Safety Land Company liabilities over thirty thousand pounds. Other companies affected. Vat you tink of him, now?

Bun. (*chuckling*). And I sold out two days before.

BLAZ. Don't you shake your handts mit yourself, but mit me. Dat was by my advice.

BUN. Yes, yes. They find it hard to catch Benjamin Bunter napping.

BLAZ. Lis'en. (*reads*). "Panic spread to Manchester and Liverpool. Lancashire Banking Association gone, Smith, Smith and Shirley gone—Brown and Brothers hard hit, and shaky."

BUN (*eagerly*). What, Brown! Brown! That's the Brown who's down here, and blocked me buying this property. Why, there's a chance now for me to get it.

BLAZ. Say we, mine frien'.

BUN. We?

BLAZ. Yah, you find de capital, und I furnish the scheme. (*gets out paper and ink on table* L.)

BUN. What are you writing?

BLAZ. The brospectus of the Cleve Abbey Coal and Hematite Iron Mining Company——

BUN. A magnificent estate——

BLAZ. Of immense coal-fields——(*writes*.)

BUN. With inexhaustible stores of iron, with railway and canal facilities within easy distance.

BLAZ. Hush! Here gomes Prown! (*he and* BUNTER *converse* L.)

Enter, R. U. E., BROWN, *busy with open letters in his hands.*

BROWN (*comes down* C., *aside*). Had these reached me in time, I might have saved—no, what could I have done ?—at least, try to stem the tide. And I was so happy here! That dream's over now. Too late! too late! They must have fifty thousand pounds, in twenty-four hours—and twelve hours have gone of them! Poor Lilly! good-by to you!

BLAZ. (*aside to* BUNTER). Now is your dime—you advance him the money—and take de mortgage of him.

BUN. (*same*). I see.

BLAZ. (*same*). Fafasour gannot bay, and de land is yours.

BUN. (*same*). Yes. (*goes to* BROWN, *who has taken a seat despondently* R.) These are awful times. Business is done for, if we do not have the confidence that should be between man and man. You are hit?

BROWN. Hard hit!

BUN. I feel for you. You have my Cher-ristian sympathy!

BROWN. It a'n't sympathy we need now, but the ready money!

BUN. Don't mock at moral support, my brother. How much do you want?

BROWN (*doubtingly*). Will you help me?

BUN. How much do you want?

BROWN. Thirty or forty thousand.

BUN. I tell you what I will do. You shall have the money down, if you transfer to me the mortgage on Cleve Abbey.

BROWN. As security?

BUN. No! I never *lend*—I buy. Forty thousand?

BROWN. It's a dead loss of five thousand! But beggars must not be choosers. Drowning men will catch at straws. I's a bargain.

BUN. (*goes to* L. *table and fills up check*). A good action is never lost. Ah! it a'n't every man who can look into his heart and his bankers' account and find forty thousand pounds to help a fellow Christian in affliction! (*rolls his eyes upwards*.)

BROWN. (*takes cheque*). Mr. Bunter, you have driven a hard bargain, but no matter. I have my work to do. If Mr. Blazenbaig will come with me to Mr. Secker, he will give him the mortgage.

[*Exit,* R. U. E. BLAZENBAIG *goes up* C. *to exit* R. U. E.

Bun. Ah, my friend, the consolation of having done a good action and relieved the unfortunate——

Blaz. Of their cash! You have cleared five thousand. Ah, dere is no one but de Christian who can get de interest like de Jew!

[*Exit*, R. U. E.

Enter, R. 1 E., Lady Mildred.

Lady M. Fanny will be here presently with her mother.

Bun. That's just the thing that weighs upon my 'eart! I can't understand Fanny. It's very hard when a father can't understand his own child. She's had the top of edication, and all the h'elevating influences that money could buy, and she does nothing but talk of 'igh art, and 'igh church, and 'igh this and that—till she gets so 'igh that she never comes down again.

Lady M. (R. C. *front*). Yes, Fanny is a little given to rhodomontade.

Bun. (C. *front*). Rhodomontade? (*puzzled*) Ye-es, rhodomontade—that's the word, my lady! And she, who could have everything new and made to order, runs after the old. Old pictures, old statues, old ruins—why, she is almost as bad as her mother about wishing for a place like this. In fact, they have so h'influenzaed me that I shouldn't mind buying it myself.

Lady M. Unfortunately, it is not in the market.

Bun. Hem! odder things than that have happened. Bless you, it could all be settled private y—and Cleve Abbey would be in new hands before you knew yourself.

Lady M. (*loftily*). Mr. Bunter!

Bun. Ah, you and I know what we know, my lady. In fact all the county knows——

Lady M. All the county may know that Mr. Vavasour, I confess, has been in trifling difficulties, but I have the pleasure to inform all the county that they are over. Mr. Brown has proposed for my daughter's hand.

Bun. Brown marry her to save the estate? (*chuckles*) Poor Brown!

Lady M. What do you mean?

Bun. That Brown hasn't a *brown* (*English for "red," "copper," "penny," in American slang*) left to bless himself with. Brown Brothers have gone up! to smash!

Lady M. Mr. Brown is a rich man! I do not understand.

Bun. I dare say he will have to part with the Cleve Abbey mortgage. I suppose you'd rather not that a stranger should come into it, so don't forget that I wouldn't mind making you an offer.

Lady M. You must be mad or intoxicated!

Bun. Madam, I never drink anything afore dinner. [*Exit*, L. 2 E.

Lady M. (*alone*) What a gulf I had nearly fallen into. Brown is not a rich man now. (*walks up and down excitedly*) At any price, Lilian's chances must be kept open.

Enter Brown, R. U. E.

Ah, Mr. Brown, I wanted to see you. I hope you have not had bad news in the letters which you have received?

Brown (R. C. *front*). The worst, my lady. I am ruined.

Lady M. Ah!

Brown. Yes, in these days of rash speculation, the innocent must suffer with the guilty. **Hard lines, hard lines!**

Lady M. Very hard.

BROWN. When I proposed to your daughter, I was a rich man. Now I have lost—you do not know all I have lost. I don't complain for that —but I cannot easily lose Lilian.

LADY M. I sympathize with you. I shall always have great respect for you. (*gives her hand*) Will you break it to her, or shall I? I think from you it would come best.

BROWN. It's a hard trial, but I will go through it. (*Exit* LADY MILDRED, L. I. E.) Yet how shall I face her, and cast a cloud upon her bright face—upon her bright heart. God bless her. (R. C. *front.*)

Enter, R. U. E., LILIAN.

LIL. (*gay'y*). Fanny is going away, but she is happy with Bertie. You are going away, and I shall have no one to be happy with. How sad you look! what has occurred to distress you? (*puts her arms on* BROWN'S *affectionately.*)

BROWN. Will you forgive me? What will you think of me when you find I am not now what I was some hours since! Lilian, I am ruined man.

LIL. (*sobered from her liveliness*). What do you mean?

BROWN. My house has gone down among the wrecks by speculations. It is through no fault of mine!

LIL. I should think not! (*embraces him.*)

BROWN. I shall save the fragments, but at a heavy sacrifice. Anyhow I must begin the world anew. To make a way in the New World, a soldier must have but his weapons, a man no encumbrances. What is your answer?

LIL. (*tearfully*). Must I answer?

BROWN. Yes, it is for you to decide. Let your whole heart speak.

LIL. What can I do? I cannot, I cannot.

Enter, R. U E., LADY MILDRED, *who overhears the following.*

BROWN. Good-by! (*takes* LILIAN'S *hand*) Think of me sometimes — for I shall think of you always.

LIL. Stay! (BROWN *returns to her, but she suddenly repulses him, half fainting*) Oh, mamma! mamma! (*sobs, and* BROWN *catches her as she falls exhausted.*)

PICTURE.

For change of tableau, LILIAN *is supported in a swoon by* LADY MILDRED, *at* C. *front. while* BROWN *is standing up* C, *as if to exit* R. U. E.

SLOW CURTAIN.

ACT III.

SCENE.—*Drawing-room in 4th grooves.*

Discover at L. *table,* BUXTER *and* SECKER, *over wine, nuts and wine-crackers.*

SECK. (*after sipping wine*). I never tasted anything more delightful.

BUN. Yes, it's worth the money. It stands me in fifteen guineas a dozen, but for a good thing I don't mind expense.

SECK. Admirable doctrine, and wine.

BUN. Well, you know, Brown held the mortgage on Cleve Abbey, and sold it to me. It was a pretty good investment for cash, and as my wife has her heart set on it I don't mind if I make an offer. I'll give eighty thousand down. You repeat this to the parties concerned, who will find it a liberal offer, and I have no doubt that you will find a fifty pun note under your plate the next time you put your legs under Benjamin Bunter's mahogany.

SECK. Really, you great capitalists have ways——

BUN. *And* means! With ways and means, *and* Cher-ristian principles, a man need stick nowhere on the road.

SECK. You evidently stick at nothing. Has Mr. Brown been here yet?

BUN. I expect him this morning to talk over our settlement. By the way, tell them that we can do it all in a sociable manner—I don't like to be hampered with lawyers——

SECK. (*drily*). Oh, you do not want lawyers about you.

BUN. I think I may consider the transaction settled. (*rises.*)

SECK. (*rises*). I have no doubt that everything will be arranged to the satisfaction of the principals concerned

BUN. Keep dark on our understanding.

SECK. Oh, I certainly am not eager to show light upon it.

[*Exit*, L. 1 E. D.

BUN. I fancy my right to Cleve Abbey is as good as the Vavasours. What pleasure to repay them for their haughtiness to me. They pretend to look down on B. B., but B. B. is too big to be frowned down.

Enter, L 1 E., BLAZENBAIG, *with papers and a black leather bag, which he puts on chair.*

BUN. Back from town, Blazen?

BLAZ. I've got the analysis of the Cleve Abbey ore.

BUN. What does the professor think of it?

BLAZ. Beautiful! He's found seventy-five per cent. of iron—ten more than I expected. I have had the map drawn out by a regular mining draughtsman. (*shows map and paper*) Dere is hundreds und hundreds in the broberty, you vas see.

BUN. (*delighted*). I wouldn't sell the estate for twice what I have offered this moment.

BLAZ. Quite right (BUNTER *tries to take map and paper*) It's all right. Keep your hands off.

BUN. What?

BLAZ. Der analysis und map are mine.

BUN. Do you hold off for terms? (R. C.)

BLAZ. (C.). Terms? Yah! Der tables was turn himself now. You und I was not shtand in dat same bosition vat ve did shoost now a leedle while zince

BUN. After the many good things we have been together in?

BLAZ. Ah! dem vas der boobles—but dis vas no booble. Dis is ein good, solid pudding, and (*empathically*) I vants meine schlice.

BUN. Do you remember what you were when I first knew you?

BLAZ. Do you remember vat *you* vas ven I first took you in der handt! und daught you to make tousands? You vas a leedle, low, crawling gontractor—mit no soul abuf p ute vorce or der figures of weekly wages to d r workingman. I daught you der philosopher' stone —der art vat cransvorm baber into gold—speculation! I daught you vinanzeering, und dey vill pild you ein grandt statue von day—all py me.

Vile you hat de leedle visch to fry—I dakes vat share you gi, me—but dis ish no sprat, but a vale, und I von't pe content mit only de blubber!

Bun. You can rely on me, you know.

Blaz. I rely on mein ownself. If you will not agree, I do not gare. I can go into der market mein ownself—dere aro lots of gapitalists who vill outpid you by five tousauds. I haf der map, und de analysis.

Bun. This is very sad, Blazy, my friend ; I did not think that you were capable of so much mistrust. It strikes a deathblow at all confidence between man and man. (*tries to take map and paper again.*)

Blaz. I will keep them.

Bun. What do you want?

Blaz. Two tousand bounds down, and half of all der profits.

Bun. But the purchase money and all the preliminary expenses will have to come out of me?

Blaz. I vill once you half!

Bun. This is cutting to the 'art. But I have not seen the analysis.

Blaz. Confidence petween man und man ! (*holds papers from* Bunter) I vill show you the table. (*lets* Bunter *see part of the paper, but no more*) Nein, nein !

Bun. Oh! how can you be so—(*goes to table,* L) It is disgusting! Not because of the money, but of the want of trust in an old friend. (*seated at table.*)

Blaz. Drust! Do you dink I vould drust mein own bruder unless he baid me in atvance—nein, nein !

Bun. (*writes*). Here is the check.

Blaz. (*takes check*). Thank you. (*reads*) "Pay—Blazenbaig—two thousand—" All right. (*gets his bag*) Now I vill geep out of de way. I haf de wish to geep mein handts glean—— [*Exit,* L. 1 E. D.

Bun. Then give me back my check ! (*aside*) Of all the rascals that I ever knew——

Enter, L. 1 E. D., Footman.

Well, sir, what do you want?

Footman. Mr. Tollit, Clerk of Works, sir.

Bun. Show him in.

Exit Footman *and enter* Tollit, L. 1 E. D.

Bun. How do, Tollit? how's Mrs. T.? not ill, I hope. I did not see her at chapel last night.

Clerk. Well, you see, sir, she was off to a little party upon the anniversary of my darter's gitting married, and she thought she might excuse herself once in a year.

Bun. I am very sorry. A neglect of Christian principles is not the way to prosper a young family. Well, what's on your mind now?

Clerk. A lot of bricks that's turned out bad, sir.

Bun. Can't be sold?

Clerk. No, sir.

Bun. Can't be used?

Clerk. No, sir.

Bun. (*hesitatingly*). What can we do with them? Oh, they are building a chapel down at the East End. Take those bricks to the Committee from me, with my blessing on the good work.

Clerk (*aside*). With bad bricks?

Bun. Thus nothing is without its use, when one is guided by Christian principles. [*Exit* Clerk, L. 1 E. D.

Enter, R. 2 E. *opening*, MRS. BUNTER.

MRS. BUNTER (*flourishing roll of parchment*). They've found it!

BUN. What? The ten-pun' note you lost the other day?

MRS. B. Our pedigree from Heralds College!

BUN. (*seated at L. table*). Heralds! Nonsense!

MRS. B. The Vavasours shan't have everythink to themselves. Do look at it – it's a perfect duck of a pedigree.

BUN. Duck? (*grumblingly*) And I'll wager it brings its bill with it.

MRS. B. A bagatelle.

BUN. How much?

MRS. B. Only one hundred and thirty pounds.

BUN. I have just had my pocket picked of two thousand pounds, and now I am to be robbed of a hundred and thirty! Am I to pay for a pack of stuff and falsehoods?

MRS. B. I am so glad that they have found our arms.

BUN. And I have found their hands in my pockets!

MRS. B. Just hear a bit of it. (*reads*) "The family of Bunter is of Anglo-Saxon origin, and came from Exeter."

BUN. Now, how did they find that out, I wonder? Well, as I have got to pay for it, I suppose I may as well look at it. (*takes paper from* MRS. BUNTER.)

MRS. B. Ain't it lovely!

BUN. "The family of Bunter is of Anglo-Saxon origin, and were tenants of the soil before the Conqueror came over, who confiscated their possessions." You see, Maria, my dear, the aristocrats were down on us even in them days. "We have no doubt that they offered a stubborn resistance to the invader." I am glad of that? "They were not prominent during the perilous times of the War of the Roses." Oh, indeed! they have only to see which side was uppermost to find where they were. "And do not appear again until the days of the Protector, when we find one Praywell Bunter the parish constable of Wrexhill." Ah! Maria, we have come down by then! "Under the reign of the three Georges they did not occupy any position of public prominence."

MRS. B. Skip that! what does it say about you, dear?

BUN. (*reads with growing delight*). "We do not hear of the name until the days of the present bearer of the title, that illustrious designer and contractor, Benjamin Bunter, Esq, of Beaumanoir Park, who is so often mentioned in connection with great public works, not only in the United Kingdom but throughout the world, who is the son of that eminent divine, the Rev. Boanerges Bunter, of Ball's Pond, Islington." Ah! that's most delicately put!

MRS. B. You don't begrudge the money now, do you?

BUN. N-no! I wonder how they found it all out.

MRS. B. And all the pretty pictures, with diamonds and spades, for all the world like a pack of playing-cards.

BUN. Well, if I accept it, it's not for myself. Dear no! but for the sake of my father! Oh! how he would have been delighted to have seen this, whether when he sat in the coal and tater shed during the week days, or stood in the pulpit on the Lord's Day—else, all this is vanity.

MRS. B. Now we won't be crowed ower by Lady Mildred.

BUN. The impudence of the woman. She has driven over, with her daughter, in the pony-carriage, just as if nothing was going to happen to take away their possession of the Abby.

MRS. B. What do you say about the sweetness between her nephew and Fanny?

Bun It's not to be thought of. The young fellow hasn't got a rap.

Mrs. B. But he may be a lord some day. Suppose the expected child should be a girl——

Bun. It may just as well be a boy. But I have prepared for that. I have bribed the doctor's confidential man, and he will telegraph to me if it is a girl. And, according to the ideas, the little event will not be long coming off.

Mrs. B. Well, I'll go and show my lady my bignonias. And I will tell Fanny that I am not sure but that she will yet find a husband in Bertie [*Exit*, R. 2 E.

Enter, L. 1 E. D., *Telegraph* MESSENGER.

Mess. A telegram sir.

Bun. (*takes telegram. Aside*). *What's this?* (*reads paper*) "You are not to give gratuities to the bearer." I was not going to (*exit* MESSENGER, L. 1 E. D.) It's from the doctor's man, "Mrs. Reginald Fitznrse of twins!" (*alarmed*) No, no; girls! (*re-assured*) Ah! The speculation looks better now! Lord Bearholm! Ahem! The next thing to being a lord one's self is being the father of one.

Enter, R. 2 E., LADY MILDRED, LILIAN, FANNY, *and* MRS. BUNTER.*

LADY M. (*with eye-gloss up*). Ah! oh! very gorgeous indeed! There is such an air of brightness and gloss of newness on each article that after the dulness of the Abbey, I am quite dazzled.

Mrs. B. Oh, if it wasn't for me, Bunter would have a new coat of paint put upon everything once a year.

LADY M. Including the pictures?

Mrs. B Ain't they lovely! That one in the corner is a real *Raffle*

LADY M. Ah! *won* at one?

Fan. (*to* LILIAN). How do you like it?

Lil. (*to* FANNY). Ah! it is much too bright for my tastes.

Fan So do I like the cold gray of ancestral ruins, too. (*she and* LILIAN *converse together up* L.)

Mrs B. And the statues—aren't they fine——

LADY M. Are they also portraits of the family?

Bun. (*aside*). These aristocrats have no taste for h'Art! (*aloud, loftily*) You see, my lady, we have to patronize the artists like the Merchant Princes of Florence and Venice. Bless you, for a real good thing, I don't mind paying any price. That's a fine bit of *shy-her-a-skewer* there —its by a R. A.

LADY M By a—I beg your pardon?

Bun By a R. A.—a R'yal Academician! (*aside*) What a damned fool this woman is!

Mrs. B. We are sure to get the tip-top cream of everything. Just look at the garden—chockfull of aviaries and stucco, and conservatories —all done by contract.

LADY M. Are the statues done by contract, too? And these (*looking about*) are the family portraits—of what time? I fancy I recognize some old friends.

Mrs. B. Oh, dear, no. They are all bran-new!

LADY M. Yet I fancied I had seen them before—in the vicinity of the New Road Ah! some Sevres and Dresden—are you so fond of *bric-a-brac*, Mr. Bunter?

*LADY MILDRED.	*MRS. B.	*BUNTER.	FANNY.	*LILIAN
R.	R. C.	C.	L. C.	L.

Bun. (*puzzled, aside*). Break a back! The woman's crazed—there ain't enough of the china to load a boy. (*aloud*) Yes, yes, I've a liking for stones and things——

Mrs. B. If they are old. Dear, yes, I could drink cheap tea if it was out of a genuine old chany bowl.

Bun. Maria, don't be ridiculous!

Lady M. Why do you call this place Beaumanoir Park—why not Bunter House?

Mrs. B. It's not sufficiently high-sounding—Beaumanoir Park has such a ring of aristocracy about it.

Lady M. And does not sufficiently indicate the owners.

[*Exit*, R. 2 E., *with* Mrs. Bunter.

Bun. (*aside*). She's a-having some sneer at me. Dreadful envious these swells are. (*exit*, L. 1 E. D. Lilian *and* Fanny *come down* C., Fanny *on* Lilian's *right*.)

Lil. No, dear, this is all too bright for me, and there's such a new look on all the furniture that I should never think of sitting down anywhere for a quiet read of Tennyson.

Fan. Ah! you shall see my oratory—all hung with black, and with such a pet of a death-head, in ivory. You must come over some day, and we will condole in it together.

Lil. I am not addicted to that sort of thing. I am much too lighthearted for that.

Fan. Ah, you should mortify yourself. Live on dry bread and water for a week. That will reduce you to a state of sweet despondency.

Lil. (*lightly*). I am afraid I should relapse into hot coffee and rolls on the slightest provocation. I have an awful appetite as well as a very light heart. And yet (*sadly*) I have more reason than you to be sad.

Fan. That is because you do not see Mr. Brown.

Lil. And so it is with you and Bertie. By the way, shall I give him your love when I see him?

Fan. (*laughing*). Thank you, I can give it myself. I see him every day. (Lilian *is surprised*.)

Enter, R., Brown.

Lil. And I do not know when I may see him.

Fan. (*seeing* Brown). But I do.

Lil. When?

Fan. Now! (Brown *comes forward*)

Lil. Mr. Brown!

Brown. I have come to see Mr. Bunter on business.

(*Voice of* Mrs. Bunter, *off* R). Fanny!

Fan. Yes, mamma!

(*Voice of* Mrs. B., *same*). Fanny!

Fan. Coming, mamma!

Lil. Mr. Brown here?

Fan. I will see that you are not disturbed!   [*Exit*, R. 2 E.

Lil. Mamma is here and I am with her. Do not look so cold. Have you lost hope? Have you no good news?

Brown. I have lost everything else, at least. It was a hard struggle, but we pulled through. It was an awful three weeks. I wonder that every hair on my head has not turned gray.

Lil. Don't laugh! (*at* C., *beside* Brown) You have come out with honor, I know. Trust to the future.

Brown. I had a future once. But that is all over. I shall not disarrange your family plans. Better for us to say the last good-by.

(*Voice of* Mrs. Buxter, R.). Miss Vavas ur.

Lil. I must speak with you.

(*Voice of* Lady Mildred, *off* R.). Lilian!

Lil. (*calls off* R.). I am coming, mamma! (*to* Brown) Stay here till I come. [*Exit*, R. 2 E.

Brown. Ah! how the sight of her warms the blood again. To leave England forever can be done—but to leave Lilian! Ah! (*pause, looks* R.) Here comes that snob! I can't face him now.

[*Exit, hurriedly,* L. 1 E. D.

Enter, R. 2 E., Buxter *and* Fanny, *to* C., Fanny *on his right.*

Bux. Why are you sulking all the time just like a girl refused a new doll? You know I don't spare any money to gratify your silly whims. Cheer up and don't look like a miser's ghost, who's been robbed of his hoard!

Fan. (*sentimentally*). Don't ask me, father to veil with smiles a breaking heart!

Bux. Be calm!

Fan. Calm? (*hysterically*) Who speaks of calm? "If any calm be there, it is a calm despair!"

Bux. Pooh, pooh! come, come, none of this nonsense! Try and be reasonable. Has this Mr. Finnurse a position?

Fan. I never thought of that.

Bux. I'll be bound you didn't.

Fan. Oh, papa! That's no fault of his. He's very handsome, and excellent in dancing.

Bux. That's not the kind of figures I want him to be clever at.

Fan. Oh! clever! he has passed the Civil Service Examination!

Bux. (*shaking his head*). Hum. I don't know about that. I never passed one myself, so I don't know what it is to pass. Well, well, just notice the time, my dear.

Fan. (*looks round*) Yes, papa.

Bux. (*aside*). They'll never think that I had a telegram with the news before the regular intelligence comes. (*aloud*) It is the hour of your happiness, for I dare say my objections to the young man will be shortly removed.

Fan. Oh, papa! (*kisses him affectedly*) Bless you! very much bless you.

Bux. (*kisses her*). Ditto! very much ditto!

Fan. Ditto? what do you mean, papa? (*surprised*)

Bux. Bless you.

Fan. Oh! (*satisfied*.)

Bux. And the sooner I see the young man, the sooner, I suppose, you will be yourself again.

Fan. That won't be long, papa! (*goes up* C.. *and waves her handkerchief at* D F.)

Bux. What's that for?

Fan. For Bertie!

Bux. What! is he there in my garden on the lookout? Do you mean to say this sort of thing would have gone on if I had not given my consent?

Fan. Yes, papa. (*comes down.*)

Bux. And do you call this honoring of your father and your mother, by *candlestine* meetings?

Fan. Is it not the best way of honoring one's father and mother to give them so good a son-in-law?

Bun. But how about his principles of piety ?

Fan, I will teach him, and guide him to the simple doctrines of the Early Church.

Bun. Oh ! (*doubtfully*) I hope he will like them !

Fan. You have made me so glad. I will go to mamma. When he comes you must treat him kindly. (*aside, going* R.) Fanny Bunter— Mrs. Bertie Fitzurse —" Plenty of cards ! "   [*Exit*, R. 2 E.

Enter, running, BERTIE, D. F.   *He comes down* L. *side.*

Ber. (*surprised to see* BUNTER). The governor ! (*stammers*) I didn't expect to see *you* here !

Bun. (*aside*). After all the edication that girl's got ! (*aloud*) Mr. Fitzurse, I understand that you wish to pay your addresses to my daughter. There are no objections to that, in this quarter.

Ber. Well, I wish I had known that before. It ain't pleasant to wait under the oak like (*hesitates*) Charles the—the Twelfth ! It's deuced uncomfortable and damp, waiting to see (*waves his handkerchief as* FANNY *waved hers*) one to come—two to go.

Enter SERVANT, L. 1 E. D.

SERVANT. Mr Brown, sir, by appointment.

Bun. You can go to join the ladies. (FITZURSE *bows and runs off* R. 2 E.)

Enter, L. 1 E. D., BROWN.

Bun. Ah! Mr. Brown ! You have had an early journey. Will you take some breakfast ? (BROWN *nods*. BUNTER *to* SERVANT) Montmorency!

SERVANT. Sir ?

Bun. Get breakfast ready for Mr. Brown. (SERVANT *bows and exits* L. 1 E. D.)

BROWN *takes papers from his bag, and he and* BUNTER *go over them at table,* L. *front.*

BROWN. There is the forty thousand pounds you lent me—that s five thousand at least that I have paid for the transaction.

Bun. Hum ! I don't know. I could have had ten *per cent.* for my money in those times.

BROWN. Will you sell me back the mortgage on the Vavasour Estate ? If so, what is the figure ?

Bun. A sale is a sale, and I never go from my principles.

BROWN. But the family is embarrassed, and the deeds are nothing but paper.

Bun. I don't look at it to expect my money to come out of the estate. I buy because I like it, so I don't mind giving a fancy price.

BROWN (*smiling to himself*). So you mean to buy ?

Bun. Yes—a private sale by arrangement between the parties won't hurt their feelings. The place is much too gloomy for me, and I am not fond of Abbeys, but Mrs. Bunter likes ruins, and she generally has her wish.

Enter, L. 1 E. D., BLAZENBAIG

Ah, Blazy, my boy ! (*to* BROWN *again*) So, after all, you see, Mr. Brown, I haven't really lost anything by obliging a friend.

BLAZ. Ah ! how are you, Prown ?

Brown. Ah, my friend, do you still give your leisure to fishing and geology?

Blaz. Yah, fishing is a fine thing for de stones. (L. C.)

Brown (*meaningly*). Some people do not know the value of stones.

Blaz. (*sharply*). Vat do you mean?

Brown. Do you remember the morning at the Abbey, when Miss Vavasour and I stopped you, and we turned the stones out of the basket? I kept a coup'e of those stones.

Blaz. Vat for?

Brown. Oh, merely out of s'mple curiosity. They were knocking about my office when a friend of mine, who is also fond of fishing and geology, suggested that I should have them analyzed.

Blaz. But you were not sooch a fool for to do that?

Brown. But I was such a fool. (Bunter *comes down* R. C., *interested*)

Blaz. And you found not'ing in de mare's nest?

Brown. I found that the land is full of ore, giving seventy-five *per cent.* of iron (*shows paper*) There's the analys s.

Bun. Pooh, pooh! I don't want to see it!

Blaz. Oh, an analysis is good for not' ng but to light der cigar.

Bun. I don't care for scientific opinion. I can buy 'em for a guinea a-piece any day. (*he takes the paper from* Brown, *and he and* Blazenbaig *look at it.*)

Brown. So you still mean to buy?

Bun. All the same, though this is some mistake.

Brown. There's no mistake. (*to* Bunter) I'll trouble you for that analysi-. *(takes paper.)*

Bun. Come, Mr. Brown, we'll do the right thing by you. If you will stand half the purchase money, you shall have a clear third of the profits.

Blaz. Nein, nein, we vill schare und schare alike!

Brown. Impossible. Though a very tempt ing offer.

Bun. Yes, take the terms and my blessing with it.

Brown. If anybody is to share, I should think the Vavasours should be let in.

Bun. Pshaw! what is it to them? There is no reservation made in the mortgage of mineral rights.

Brown. There may be no legal claims of theirs, but surely, between gentlemen——

Bun. What's that got to do with *us?* I am very well satisfied with the law. I don't want to put nonsense in the place of business.

Brown. That would be sinful! It is such reasonings as these that has made the name of British merchants a by-word, and made British industry stand still in the pillory with the brand of speculation on its forehead!

Bun. I had great respect for you, Mr. Brown, but your sentiments amaze me—they are not such as beseem the man of business.

Enter Servant, L. 1 E. D., *with tray of breakfast things*

Servant. Mr. Brown, breakfast, sir. (L)

Bun. Take it into the breakfast-room. Montmorency, you need not wait. (*exit* Servant, L. 3 E. D., *to* Brown) Honor b.ight, you won't mention the find to the Vavasours?

Brown. I will not. I leave you to reconcile your practice of pious principles with your professions.

[*Exit,* L. 3 E. D. Blazenbaig *goes up and locks* L. 3 E. D.

Bun. What's that for?

Blaz. I vill make him safe. (Bunter *takes seat at l. table and hides his face in one hand*) Vat is de madder? can it pe that you vas plushing?

Bun. I thought once as Brown did.

Blaz. Put you haf t'ought petter of it now.

Enter, r. 2 e., Lady Mildred *and* Lilian.

Lady Mildred. Ah, Mr. Bunter! I have been admiring the many beauties of your lovely place.

Bun. (*aside*). The hypocrite! who'd think she had a heavy mortgage hanging over her head?

Lady M. Here comes our legal adviser.

Enter, r. 2 e., Secker *and* Vavasour.

Vavasour (*rubbing his hands cheerily*). A nice, brisk, hearty morning. (All *go to table,* l.)

Bun. (*taking seat*). Mr. Secker has told you of the offer I have made for Cleve Abbey?

Vav. Yes. Very liberal, I think.

Bun. I don't think we shall want the lawyers in. It only adds to the expenses. (*to* Secker) No off'nce, of course? (Secker *smiles and bows.*)

Lady M. Oh, no! then every paragraph is a guinea, and every sentence six and-eightpenc . It is perfectly useless. (Vavasour *and* Secker *get parchments and deeds ready for signing.*)

Seck. Oh, you don't want anything to do with the lawyers, eh?

Bun. I have offered eighty thousand pounds for Cleve Abbey. I don't think there is any occasion to go into particulars?

Lady M. It is perfectly unnecessary.

Vav. Here is the release and the money for the mortgage, principal and interest.

Bun. Wh-what do you mean?

Vav. It will be easy for you to be one of the first to reply to some scandalous whisperings originated against my credit, by learning that we are fully prepared (*shows bank-bills*) to meet all charges in clearing off the mortgage.

Blaz. Po'ztausend!

Bun. Then y u are not in want of money?

Vav. You will be de delighted to hear that Cleve Abbey has been found to be one vast field of rich hematite iron. Mr. Secker has found a capitalist who will not only pay off the mortgage, but advance five times the sum on a new mortgage. This does not include the money accuring from royalties from permission to mining companies which may be formed.

Bun. A delusion! there's not so much iron ore in the land as in my grounds.

Vav. Perhaps Mr. Blazenbaig, as your geologist and scentific adviser, may like to look at the analysis? (*shows paper.*)

Bun. I don't want to see any analysises! They're all moonshine!

Seck. It's from the same professor that drew up a simila report for Mr. Blazenbaig!

Lady M. (*rises*). We thought that you ought to be the first to hear of our good fortune, as one of your Christian princ ples could not fail to rejoice at such good tidings from another.

Bun. (*aside*). I hate that woman! (*aside to* Blazenbaig) It's that fellow Brown that has let them in for the good thing. That's the reason he wouldn't go in with us. (*aloud*) I see, you have been told of this by Mr. Brown.

VAV. Mr. Brown! I have not heard his name mentioned in connection with such a matter.

LADY M. Mr. Secker may inform you, though he will not tell us.

SECK. Not at present. (*to* BUNTER, *pointedly*) I would not tell you, no not if I were to find a fifty-pound note under my plate!

BUN. I have not been fairly treated in this affair. (*gives mortgage and receives money*) I may say I have not been legally dealt with! An agreement to sell was made, and that is as good as a sale any day—in equity!

LADY M. I think, Mr. Bunter, that the less there is said about equity in the transaction, the better! Come along, Lilly! we'll go to Mrs. Bunter, and see the flowers.

VAV. And I will go, too, to see if there is any novelty that may give us a hint for the redecoration of the Abbey. (*going* R.) That is the use of these new houses—they give us the results of experienced furnishers. (*to* BUNTER) Experiments in *corpori vila*! you know! I beg your pardon, you *don't* know! (R. 2 E.)

BUN. (*aside*). They shan't see that I am down in the mouth. (*aloud, going to* L. 1 E. D.) I shall go to my lawyer and see if I am to be choused in this artful way! (*at* L. 1 E) I repeat the word, madam, choused!
                                                    [*Exit*, L. 1 E. D.

BLAZ. (*aside*). Tings begin to look vischy! I haf de cheque safe—I vill go and get him gashed at the Gounty Pank!   [*Exit*, L. 1 E. D.

LADY M. Ah! this is indeed joy! To see the fancied triumph of these insolent people growing and then to crush it in the bloom! Now we will resume our place at the head of the county families, and Lilian will enjoy the reality of the future that I dreamed of for her!
                                                    [*Exit*, R. 2 E.

VAV. (*to* LILIAN). Your mother don't try to find out to whom we owe this fortunate discovery.

LIL. Mamma is too happy for that. (*exit* VAVASOUR, R. 2 E.) I told Mr. Brown to wait for me here. I wonder where he is?

BROWN (*within* L. 3 E.). Lilian! Lilian!

LIL. Mr. Brown's voice. Where are you? (*goes* L.)

BROWN (*same*). Here in this room. The key is on your side. (LILIAN *unlocks door, and* BROWN *comes forth*.)

LIL. What are you doing there?

BROWN. Watching you through the keyhole till you were alone.

LIL. But why were you locked up in that room?

BROWN. For fear I might spoil sport.

LIL. I don't understand. Then you have heard all?

BROWN. I know of the change in your position. You are wealthy now, while I am so poor that I have to begin the world again.

LIL. Alone?

BROWN. Yes. To make one's way in a new world, a pioneer must have no sort of incumbrance. Our house must be built up again, and I am going to establish a branch in Australia.

LIL. So far away?

BROWN. It must be. I can be happy nowhere from you, but perhaps less unhappy at a distance.

LIL. I will go with you.

BROWN. No! You are not born to share a struggling man's existence. I am too poor now.

LIL. You are not as poor as I was when I loved you, and was **loved for myself alone**.

Enter, R. 2 E., LADY MILDRED.

LIL. If there are hardships, let me bear my part of them. I am prepared to live the life you have to lead.

BROWN. No. Better for us to say good-by, and not prolong discussion. Come, take courage. You have everything now to make your path pleasant. Let me toil on in the rugged road.

LIL. No! I will go with you.

LADY M. (*comes down,* C.). Lilian! Mr. Brown! (*to* BROWN) I thought, sir, that you had too much delicacy to see my daughter again after you had promised me that you would go.

LIL. Mamma! Mr. Brown is not to b'ame. It is I. I love him so dearly, mamma. (*goes to* LADY MILDRED.)

Enter VAVASOUR *and* SECKER, R. 2 E.

SECKER. Oh! are you here, Brown? I have been looking everywhere for you. My lady, here is the gentleman to whom is due all credit for the discovery of the mine on your estate, and for the raising of the money applied to relieving it of the mortgage.

LADY M., VAV. *and* LIL. Mr. Brown!

SECK. Come come, don't deny it.

BROWN. I don't deny it. (*severely*) But I thought you had more taste than to reveal what I wished kept secret for a time.

LIL. Until you were beyond our power to repay? Is it so? Oh, mamma, you cannot now refuse anything to this most generous of men? Papa, speak for me.

VAV. I think—I say, I think—he may claim his own property.

LADY M. I suppose I must give my consent. Yet I could have wished her another future.

LIL. None more happy, mamma!

VAV. I am sure you will have the best husband in the world. (*unites the hands of* LILIAN *and* BROWN) Heaven bless you—that is, if my lady has no objections.

Enter, L. 1 E. D., BUNTER.

BUN. (*aside*). The law can't help me. (*aloud*) Brown out of the room. I thought you were at breakfst.

BROWN. In the lock-up? I had a traitor on the right side of the door. (*draws* LILIAN *to him affectionately.*)

LADY M. I have the pleasure to announce to you that Mr. Brown will be the manager of the Cleve Abbey Mining Company which will be organized shortly after his marriage with my daughter.

BUN. Oh!

Enter, R. 2 E., FANNY *and* BERTIE. *with* MRS. BUNTER, *who has a paper in her hand.*

MRS. B. Here, Benjamin, a telegram for you.

BUN. (*delighted*). And, my dear lady, I have the pleasure to announce to you a marriage in my family. My daughter Fanny and Mr. Fitzurse, soon to be Lord Bearho me, it appears.

LADY M. How is that?

BUN. (*reads telegram*). "Mrs. Reginald Fitzurse has been brought to bed of two girls"—girls!

LADY M. Girls! Ah! I sincerely condole with you on the disappointment.

Bun. (*puzzled*). Disappointment! Condole! You mean, congratulate me?

Lady M. I mean what I say.

Bun. What, won't he be a lord?

Enter Blazenbaig, L. 1 E. D.

Lady M. No! You can't be expected to understand these things. (*to* Vavasour) Marmaduke, my dear, will you please to explain.

Vav. I am always called upon to explain when there is anything disagreeable.*

Vav. The baronetcy being settled on the direct line, the default of male issue only makes the right of descent fall to the next of the kin.

Bun. Then he won't be a lord after all?

Vav. No! (*bows apologetically to* Bertie) unless he is one by nature!

Bun. Done Brown! (*to* Blazenbaig) What are you snickering about? My fine fellow, I'll make you laugh the other side of your mouth. When I found the spec. looked black, I sent to stop the cheque.

Blaz. Yah, I t'ought you vould, and so I went und got him gashed first!

Bun. Done Brown again!

Vav. Let me congratulate you!

Bun. This from you, whom I always considered as a friend.

Blaz. Gonfidence petween man and man, you know!

Vav. Come, Mr. Bunter, make the best of it. Let the young folks be happy.

Ber. Ya-as! we'll make a double match of it, and enter them to be walked over the course the same day.

Mrs. B. He's such a clever young man, Bunter.

Bun. Well, I have no objections. I have learnt a lesson by it.

Lady M. So have I.

Lil. And yours is the better, mamma.

Lady M. That it does not take Old Acres——

Lil. To make New Men (*slight pause while she gives her hand proudly to* Brown) gentlemen!

Picture.

Vavasour.* *Lady M.   Mrs. B.* *Bunter.
Secker.*   Bertie.* *Fanny. Lilian.* *Brown. *Blaz.

CURTAIN.

---

* Bertie.   * Fanny.   * Lilian.   * Brown.
* Secker.   * Lady M.   * Vava.   * Bunter. * Mrs. Bunter.   * Blazenbaig.

TIME IN REPRESENTATION—TWO AND ONE-HALF HOURS.

SYNOPSIS.

MARMADUKE VAVASOUR, representative of a very old family, is a man of haughty ideas, having the misfortune to encumber his estate to such a degree that the Cleve Abbey, his manorial residence, is on the point of being sold at the very period appointed for bringing out his daughter, Miss LILIAN VAVASOUR, in London society. LADY MILDRED VAVASOUR, who is the managing head of the house, undertakes to procrastinate the calamity through inviting MR. JAMES BROWN, the holder of the mortgage, to visit the Abbey. He had previously been introduced to Miss LILIAN VAVASOUR, at a ball, and LADY MILDRED conceives that a matrimonial alliance between him and their daughter might re-establish the financial condition of the family. BROWN arrives, a simple methodical merchant, and is shortly followed by the BUNTER family, a race of parvenus, who are tolerably well received on account of their money. MRS. BUNTER informs LILIAN of her father's embarrassment and she, in turn, requests BROWN, in the event of his purchase of the house and grounds, he would conserve certain peculiarities which she especially admired. To this the merchant agrees, while BUNTER and a mining engineer discover traces of mineral wealth on the estate, bestowing upon it an immense value. The engineer pretends that he is engaged in fishing, but BROWN cleverly penetrates this fallacy, and secures some of the specimens of ore the man has covertly collected. Encouraged by LADY MILDRED, BROWN progresses favorably in his suit with LILIAN, while the scheming lady seeks to bring about a match between Miss BUNTER and BERTIE FITZURSE, a rather stupid young gentleman but presumptive heir to a title, supposed to entertain an affection for LILIAN. During the continuance of BROWN's visit, telegraphic dispatches are received announcing a commercial panic at Liverpool, and the threatened failure of BROWN's house, which would collapse, were not fifty thousand pounds to be forthcoming in the course of twenty-four hours. At the instigation of the mining engineer, BUNTER, actuated, as he states, by Christian charity, offers to advance the sum required by BROWN, taking good care, however, to pocket five thousand pounds through transfer of the mortgage on the VAVASOUR estate to himself. The change in BROWN's financial condition works a radical alteration in LADY MILDRED's matrimonial project, and the aristocratic dame suggests that he should break the news to LILIAN, and thereby effectively preclude the possibility of their union. BROWN accepts the situation and announces his intention of departing to seek his fortune in the New World. LILIAN, who has commenced sincerely to admire the merchant, promises to think of him sometimes and parts with him in sorrow. Six weeks after the purchase of the mortgage, MR. BUNTER resolves upon its foreclosure, designing to purchase the estate himself, his engineer having caused the land to be surveyed and specimens of the ores to be analyzed. He is first visited by his lawyer and subsequently by BROWN, who offers to repurchase the mortgage. BUNTER refuses, whereupon VAVASOUR enters upon the scene with his wife and daughter, tenders money in payment of the mortgage and demands a release. BUNTER, chop-fallen and swindled by his engineer, is compelled to remove the lien, when he is informed that discovery of the mineral wealth had been made by BROWN, who had, moreover, raised the money to remove the mortgage and organize a mining company, of which, after his marriage with LILIAN, he is to become the superintendent.

☞ Please notice that nearly all the Comedies, Farces and Comediettas in the following List of "DE WITT'S ACTING PLAYS" are very suitable for representation in small Amateur Theatres and on Parlor Stages, as they need but little extrinsic aid from complex scenery or expensive costumes. They have attained their deserved popularity by their droll situations, excellent plots, great humor and brilliant dialogues, no less than by the fact that they are the most perfect in every respect of any edition of plays ever published either in the United States or Europe, whether as regards purity of text, accuracy and fullness of stage directions and scenery, or elegance of typography and clearness of printing.

** In ordering please copy the figures at the commencement of each piece, which indicate the number of the piece in "DE WITT'S LIST OF ACTING PLAYS."

☞ Any of the following Plays sent, postage free, on receipt of price—*Fifteen Cents* each.

☞ The figure following the name of the Play denotes the number of Acts. The figures in the columns indicate the number of characters—M. male; F. female.

DE WITT'S ACTING PLAYS.—Continued.

DE WITT'S DRAWING-ROOM OPERETTAS.

☞ TO MUSICAL AMATEURS. ☜

The number of *Musical Amateurs*, both ladies and gentlemen, is not only *very large*, but is *constantly increasing*, and very naturally, for there is no more *refined* and *pleasant* mode of spending *leisure hours* than in *singing* and *playing* the choice productions of the best Composers. Hitherto there has been an *almost total luck of suitable pieces* adapted to *an evening's entertainment* in Parlors by Amateurs. Of course whole Operas, or even parts of Operas, require orchestral accompaniments and full choruses to give them effect, and are therefore clearly unfit for Amateur performance, while a succession of songs lacks the interest given by a plot and a contrast of characters. In this series (*a list of which is given below*) we have *endeavored to supply this want*. *The best Music of popular Composers* is wedded to appropriate words, and the whole dovetailed into plots that are effective as mere *petite* plays, but are rendered doubly interesting by the *appropriate and beautiful Music, specially arranged for them.*

LIST OF DE WITT'S MUSICAL PLAYS.
PRICE 15 CENTS EACH.

LEAP YEAR.—A Musical Duality. By ALFRED B. SEDGWICK. Music selected and adapted from OFFENBACH's celebrated Opera, "*Genevieve de Brabant.*" One Male, one Female Character.

THE TWIN SISTERS.—Comic Operetta, in One Act. The Music selected from the most popular numbers in LE COCQ's celebrated Opera Bouffe, "*Giroflé Girofla,*" and the Libretto written by ALFRED B. SEDGWICK. Two Male, Two Female Characters.

SOLD AGAIN AND GOT THE MONEY.—Comic Operetta, in One Act. The Music composed and the Libretto written by ALFRED B. SEDGWICK. Three Male, One Female Character.

THE QUEEREST COURTSHIP.—Comic Operetta, in One Act. The Music arranged from OFFENBACH's celebrated Opera, "*La Princesse de Trebizonde,*" and the Libretto written by ALFRED B. SEDGWICK. One Male, One Female Character.

ESTRANGED.—An Operetta, in One Act. The Music arranged from VERDI's celebrated Opera, "*Il Trovatore,*" and the Libretto adapted by ALFRED B. SEDGWICK. Two Male, One Female Character.

CIRCUMSTANCES ALTER CASES.—Comic Operetta, in One Act. The music composed and the Libretto written by ALFRED B. SEDGWICK. One Male, One Female Character.

MY WALKING PHOTOGRAPH.—Musical Duality, in One Act. The Music arranged from LE COCQ's Opera, "*La Fille de Madame Angot,*" and the Libretto written by ALFRED B. SEDGWICK. One Male, One Female Character.

A SINGLE MARRIED MAN—Comic Operetta, in One Act. The Music arranged from OFFENBACH's celebrated Opera Bouffe, "*Madame l'Archiduc,*" and the Libretto written by ALFRED B. SEDGWICK. Six Male, Two Female Characters.

MOLLY MORIARTY.—An Irish Musical Sketch, in One Act. The Music composed and the Dialogue written by ALFRED B. SEDGWICK. One Male, one Female Character. Suitable for the *Variety* Stage.

THE CHARGE OF THE HASH BRIGADE.—A Comic Irish Musical Sketch. The Music composed and the Libretto written by JOSEPH P. SKELLY. Two Male, two Female Characters. Suitable for the *Variety* Stage.

GAMBRINUS, KING OF LAGER BEER.—A Musical Ethiopian Burlesque, in One Act. Music and Dialogue by FRANK DUMONT. Eight Male, one Female Character. Suitable for the *Ethiopian Stage*.

AFRICANUS BLUEBEARD.—A Musical Ethiopian Burlesque, in One Act. Music and Dialogue by FRANK DUMONT. Four Male, four Female Characters. Suitable for the *Ethiopian Stage*.

A COMPLETE DESCRIPTIVE CATALOGUE OF DE WITT'S ACTING PLAYS AND DE WITT'S ETHIOPIAN AND COMIC DRAMAS, containing Plot, Costume, Scenery, Time of Representation, and all other information, mailed free and post paid on application. Address

DE WITT, Publisher,
33 Rose Street, New York.